**'Why are y**

'Are you follo
ruin my peace

'Of course I am, but then you wouldn't expect anything else, would you?' Nick shrugged. 'And I wouldn't want to disappoint you.'

'Why spare my feelings now? You never bothered to in the past.'

Nick clenched his jaw, before relaxing and allowing his lips to curve into a teasing smile. 'Bitterness, Mallory? Or perhaps...regrets?'

**Lucy Clark** began writing romance in her early teens and immediately knew she'd found her 'calling' in life. After working as a secretary in a busy teaching hospital, she turned her hand to writing medical romance. She currently lives in Adelaide, Australia, and has the desire to travel the world with her husband. Lucy largely credits her writing success to the support of her husband, family and friends.

**Recent titles by the same author:**

POTENTIAL HUSBAND

# MOTHER TO BE

BY
LUCY CLARK

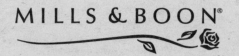

MILLS & BOON®

To Peter, Melanie and Austin—my family.
With thanks to Elizabeth, Glen, Ruth, Yvonne and Kathy
for helping me to 'get it right'. Acts 10:2

*All the characters in this book have no existence outside the imagination
of the author, and have no relation whatsoever to anyone bearing the
same name or names. They are not even distantly inspired by any
individual known or unknown to the author, and all the incidents are
pure invention.*

*First published in Great Britain 2000
Harlequin Mills & Boon Limited,
Eton House, 18-24 Paradise Road, Richmond, Surrey TW9 1SR*

© Lucy Clark 2000

ISBN 0 263 82245 1

*Set in Times Roman 10½ on 11½ pt.
03-0007-52785*

*Printed and bound in Spain
by Litografia Rosés, S.A., Barcelona*

# CHAPTER ONE

'ONE...two...three...four...five. Breathe,' Mallory instructed as she continued the compression on her patient's chest. 'Pulse?' she asked Stan, not stopping her actions for one second. When you were trying to save a life seconds counted.

'Nothing.' Stan breathed into their patient's mouth once again on Mallory's instruction, looking conscientiously for any vital signs. Stan and Mallory had worked together for the past two years as part of the Appleton General Hospital's retrieval team. Situations such as these were their biggest tests.

'Breathe,' Mallory called again. 'One...two...three...'

'Pulse!' Stan pressed two fingers to the carotid pulse. 'It's faint but it's there.'

'Status, Jeremy?' she asked another member of her team as she stopped the cardiac massage.

'The bleeding to the right leg has been stopped and is secure with a tourniquet.'

'Good. Kate,' Mallory instructed the final member of the retrieval team, 'get that oxygen mask onto him. Stan, I need BP and further pulse count. Torch.' She held out her hand and Jeremy placed it firmly in her palm.

Mallory closed her fingers around it and flicked it on with her thumb. Lifting the eyelids of her patient, she checked the pupils.

'Pupils are reacting and are the same size, so we can assume there's no internal bleeding in the brain. Report, Stan.'

'BP is one hundred over fifty. Pulse is getting stronger—fifty beats per minute.'

'Right. Now that he's stable, I'll put a neck brace on before I splint and bandage his broken arm, then he's ready for the stretcher. How long since you called for the ambulance, Kate?'

'Ten minutes. I'm expecting it—' The wail of sirens could be heard in the distance. 'Very soon,' Kate finished.

'Splint,' Mallory ordered, and with the help of Stan and Jeremy she immobilised their patient's arm. 'He'll need to be seen by an orthopaedic surgeon and treated with open reduction and fixation with plates and screws as it doesn't feel like a clean break. OK. Let's move him.'

The ambulance arrived only seconds after the patient had been secured on the stretcher. Mallory briefed the paramedics, before handing the man over into their care. Once the ambulance doors had closed the applause began.

The onlookers, who had been kept away by the barriers, clapped and some even whistled.

'Well done, Dr Newman.' Dr Osborne, one of the adjudicators, came to shake her hand. 'If you wouldn't mind delivering the verbal report, we can conclude your proceedings.'

'Thank you, Dr Osborne.' Mallory took a deep breath and looked out at the crowd. She held up her hands for silence and the applause died down. 'I'm Dr Mallory Newman, General Practitioner from Appleton on the Sunshine Coast of Queensland. This is…' she indicated her team '…RN Kate Jenkins, RN Jeremy Sampson and RN Stan MacGuire, all of whom have trained long and hard in trauma management retrieval procedures.'

There was another round of clapping. Mallory applauded her team as well, then waited for silence.

'Let me state here and now that our patient today was a volunteer from the Brisbane Drama Institute and did a superb acting job. He is perfectly fit and healthy and we thank him for his part in our exercise.'

More clapping. 'Today we were faced with an accident victim who had sustained a fractured right humerus, which is the bone above the elbow, a severe laceration to the left thigh which involved damaged muscle tissue and a damaged femoral artery, a minor concussion and most importantly, our patient had stopped breathing.

'First we stabilised his breathing by performing cardio-pulmonary resuscitation and expired air resuscitation. Once the breathing had been restored, oxygen was given to the patient to assist in relaxed, controlled breathing. A swollen lump at the rear of the skull indicated the possibility of a head injury but, because the pupils reacted to light and hadn't changed in size, only a minor concussion was diagnosed. A neck brace was secured around the patient's neck to keep his head as still as possible.

'The bleeding of the femoral artery was stabilised with a tourniquet and now awaits further medical attention by a specialist at the nearest hospital. The right arm had minor bruises and abrasions, and upon examination I concluded the bone was probably broken in at least two places. An X-ray at the nearest hospital would be required to confirm this and, if so, treatment by an orthopaedic surgeon would be necessary.

'When the patient was handed over to the paramedics his breathing, blood pressure and pulse were all stable. His injuries were stable. Without the tight teamwork exhibited here today, the patient could easily have stopped breathing or have bled to death. First aid is a valuable asset for each and every person. Please,' she implored, 'sign up for a course. The Brisbane General Hospital, which has sponsored this Retrieval Team Performance Techniques Week, can answer any questions you have regarding courses.

'I'd like to thank you all for your co-operation in being so unobtrusive during our retrieval team's examination.'

The round of applause was deafening and when she looked at the adjudicators, who had circled them as they'd worked—scribbling notes on their clipboards—they were all clapping, too.

'Well done again, Dr Newman,' Dr Osborne reiterated. 'Your team has worked marvellously and your speech was not only clear and concise but in terms the general public could understand. From checking the preliminary scores of the other adjudicators, I'd say you're in the lead, and with only one more retrieval team to perform, you're in with a good chance.'

'Thank you, Dr Osborne.' Mallory shook his hand and smiled. As she walked over to her team she glimpsed, out of the corner of her eye, a tall man with jet black hair coming through the barrier gate, headed towards them.

Turning her head sharply in his direction, she recognised him immediately. It had been five years—*five painful years*—since she'd last seen him, and Nicholas Sterling looked even better than her memory recalled. She felt her stomach tighten in anticipation of hearing his deep, rich voice.

He was wearing navy trousers, a white shirt with rolled-up cuffs, a colourful tie and dark sunglasses. Mallory didn't need to be told what colour his eyes were. She'd looked into them too many times and lost herself in their depths. Blue. The most compelling and hypnotic blue she'd ever seen. In fact, it wasn't just his eyes which had been compelling and hypnotic!

Shaking the memory from her head, Mallory hardened her resolve, surprised and annoyed that she'd turned to mush at the mere sight of him.

'You guys ready to go?' she asked her team as she

tucked a stray strand of hair back into the tight bun at the nape of her neck. 'I'm so thirsty.'

'Yeah,' Stan chided good-naturedly. 'Must put severe stress on the vocal cords, barking out orders all the time.' Stan had moved to Appleton almost five years previously and had been a valuable member of the hospital staff ever since. Having just celebrated his fifty-fifth birthday, one year after losing his wife to breast cancer, Stan had thrown himself into his nursing career.

Jeremy was his twenty-two-year old nephew and had come to live with his uncle six months before having just completed his degree. His brown eyes matched his uncle's and the two of them had formed a family unit as neither had any other living relatives.

'Well, if you're not ready to go—I'll meet you back at the car.' She turned and had only taken a few steps when a warm hand fell heavily on her shoulder. Too late, she thought.

The hand turned her around to face him. 'Leaving already? Not planning on saying hello to an…old friend?' Nick raised his eyebrows suggestively as he said the last two words.

When Mallory didn't answer he introduced himself to her team. 'Nick Sterling.'

'*The* Nick Sterling?' Kate asked incredulously. Mallory groaned at Kate's automatic response to stick her chest out even further than it did naturally. The thirty-something blonde was out hunting and was sizing Nick up as prey.

'I see my reputation has preceded me,' he said with a smile, and Kate fluttered her eyelashes at him.

'Appleton, for all its expansion over the years, is a small country town compared to Brisbane,' Stan explained. 'The rumours and gossip never stop.'

'So I see,' Nick replied with a hint of humour in his

voice. 'You haven't been telling stories about me again, have you, Mal?'

Mallory was speechless. Not only that, she was seething with annoyance and anger at his high-handed attitude. Trying desperately to control her temper in front of her colleagues, she raised her chin defiantly, before saying, 'Me? I have no need to say anything, Nicholas. The credit for the gossip that still circulates around Appleton lies solely with yourself.' There, she'd managed to hold onto her temper. Good girl, Mallory.

She took a few steps further away from him and said to her team, 'We'd better get going. If we don't report in to the hospital soon, they may start deducting marks.' Although it wasn't true, she needed some excuse to get away from Nick, and the sooner the better.

'You won't lose any marks,' Nick replied, his grin indicating he knew exactly what Mallory was trying to do.

'How do you know?' Kate asked.

'I'm one of the specialists involved in putting this programme together,' Nick told them.

'The concepts were well devised,' Stan remarked.

'Very challenging,' Jeremy pitched in.

'Does the winning team get taken out to dinner?' Kate gushed, eyeing Nick suggestively. Mallory felt ill. How dared he encourage her?

She watched as Nick gave Kate his most perfect smile, one guaranteed to melt the toughest of hearts and which he'd used on Mallory herself too many times to remember.

'An excellent idea. Dinner for the winning team. I assume you're all available tonight?' Nick received three affirmative replies, before looking at Mallory. 'Are you available tonight, Mal?' The *double entendre* wasn't lost on her but she refused to acknowledge it.

'Aren't we all being a little too presumptuous?' she felt compelled to point out. She didn't like the way Kate was

looking at Nick or, more to the point, the way Nick seemed
to be encouraging the nurse. Even though it had been almost eighteen months since his wife had died, that was still
no excuse for his behaviour.

'There's still another retrieval team to perform this afternoon. They could well knock us out of first place, if
we're even in it to begin with. The final scores are still
being tallied.'

'Mallory's right.' Nick nodded and Mallory breathed a
sigh of relief. 'But why don't we go out to dinner, regardless?'

Mallory closed her eyes, trying to block out the warmth
of his voice as it washed over her. This was turning into a
nightmare and one she'd rather not be in.

'We can talk over old times,' Nick continued. 'See if we
know some of the same people. Tell me the gossip about
myself and I'll tell you if it's accurate,' he teased, and they
all laughed. Everyone but Mallory.

All she wanted to do was to get as far away from Nicholas Sterling as possible. Her head began to pound with the
beginnings of a bad headache and she knew who was responsible for it.

'What do you say to that idea, Mallory?' Nick asked ,
his eyes all but daring her to refuse.

'I think it's a great idea,' she said without enthusiasm.
'Unfortunately, I need to return this afternoon. Taking the
day off to come down here, it's left me behind in my paperwork.'

'Surely it can wait for a few more hours?' Kate suggested. 'I mean, how often do we get to come down to
Brisbane and to be treated to dinner by such a handsome
specialist?'

'How often, indeed?' Mallory agreed, the pounding increasing by the second. 'Please, stay and enjoy yourselves.
After I've checked in with the hospital, I'll head back.'

'But, Mallory—' Jeremy protested, but she cut him off.

'Go. Have a good time. Now, if you'll excuse me.' She didn't wait for any further comments but turned and walked away. She didn't care whether they thought she was being rude or not. Nick Sterling was having a devastating effect on her equilibrium and she desperately needed to put some distance between them.

'Today I think I'll have…' Mallory surveyed the mouth-watering row of different fudges, trying to decide '…peppermint chocolate.'

'Coming right up.' Brittany cut the fudge and placed it into the mixer. This was Mallory's favourite time of the day. She watched as Brittany operated the machine that would mix the ice cream with the fudge, producing the most scrumptious tastes Mallory had ever experienced.

'There you go.' Brittany handed over the small bowl filled with the dessert. 'I'll just put it on your account.'

'Thanks.' Mallory eyed the glass dish she now held protectively in her hand. For the tourists the shop used papers containers and plastic spoons, but as this was the way Mallory treated herself she wanted it to taste the best it possibly could. Besides, in providing her own dish, she was helping the environment.

As always, she would have at least one spoonful before leaving the shop. She swirled the spoon around the edge of the bowl and scooped some up. Her lips parted in anticipation and the spoon slipped between them.

Mallory closed her eyes. 'Mmm.' She could feel her body begin to relax from the pressures of her rigorous medical practice. 'Heaven!' The texture of the small pieces of the fudge mixed with the smooth, creamy ice cream as she swirled them around in her mouth, before swallowing, always had this soothing affect on her.

Brittany laughed. 'Enjoy. I'll see you later.' She moved off to serve some other customers.

As Mallory stepped out of the shop she heard one of the customers saying, 'What was she eating? It looked delicious.'

Taking slow steps, she placed another spoonful into her mouth, then stopped at the kerb to enjoy the flavours. There were at least thirty different varieties of fudge and Mallory had sampled each and every one of the them at least fifty times over.

There were still a lot of tourists around, although the numbers would triple when summer returned. A man, pushing a pram with a toddler in it, and his pregnant wife walked on the opposite side of the road, enjoying the scenery in a leisurely fashion. His wife looked midway through her pregnancy and a pang of envy ripped through Mallory.

She scooped another spoonful of ice cream into her mouth, willing the sensations to calm the feeling of emptiness she'd carried with her for the past five years. Never would she be able to give birth to a child naturally.

She looked up to check for traffic on Appleton's busy main street, before crossing the road.

Then she saw him.

In disbelief she watched as he waved to someone in a store, then entered Peter McPhee's real estate office. What was he doing back here?

Her breath caught in her throat and the spark of desire she despised, surged through her body. It was soon overpowered by her intense dislike and anger for the man. Nick Sterling had no business being back in Appleton.

It had been six months since the retrieval team had, indeed, won the competition and Mallory had refused Nick's dinner invitation. Why was he here? Perhaps he'd decided to pursue Kate and date her. After all, the nurse was a very attractive woman.

Feeling her stomach knot in tension at the mere thought of Kate with Nick, Mallory forced herself to push the scenario from her mind. They could do whatever they wanted. She wasn't Nick's keeper.

Suzannah had been Nick's keeper. For three years Suzannah had been Nick's wife, until her death two years ago. Mallory shook her head as the painful memories came flooding back. Suzannah, who'd been captivated by Nick since she'd first set eyes on him. Nick was five years older than them and had been in his final year at high school. He'd flirted shamelessly with her and Suzannah, encouraging them in their infatuation.

Then he'd gone to medical school in Brisbane. As Mallory's older brother, Jeff, was a good friend of Nick's and was also at medical school, Nicholas Sterling had remained uppermost in her fantasies, as well as Suzannah's.

Poor, unfortunate Suzannah. Mallory shook her head sadly. A car horn beeped, bringing her out of her reverie. She looked at the occupant of the car, who was waving to her, and automatically waved back. Crossing the street, she walked up the paved pathway to the doors of the medical centre. After they'd whooshed open, Mallory continued walking through the lobby to her consulting rooms. Pushing open the glass door, she was met by her ever-smiling receptionist, Sandi.

'You'll never guess who was just in here?' she gushed as Mallory placed her bowl on the desk top.

'The King of Persia?' she growled, preoccupied with her anger. Now she had one more thing to add to her dislike of 'him'. One glimpse of Nick Sterling and she'd lost all her enjoyment of the confection she loved so much. She spooned some into her mouth, hoping to recapture the sensation again.

'Oh, what flavour did you get today?' Sandi asked, eyeing the greenish tinge to the ice cream. 'Peppermint chocolate,' she guessed before Mallory could say a word. 'I thought you had that last week?'

'Does it matter?' Mallory snapped, then immediately apologised. 'I'm sorry, Sandi. When's my next patient due?'

'You've got another ten minutes before Mrs Spock comes in.'

'That's not a nice thing to say about Mrs Koos,' Mallory chastised, but allowed the corners of her mouth to twitch into a smile.

'Well, she does look a bit Vulcanish with her dark colouring and I swear I can see the tops of her ears poking out through her hair.'

Shaking her head, Mallory walked through to her office and put the bowl on her desk. 'Coffee?' she asked Sandi.

'Sure, if you're getting some.'

'Hey, I've got ten whole minutes to spare. I've got the best dessert in the world sitting on my desk. I may as well go the entire way and have a hot cup of coffee, instead of skolling a lukewarm one.'

'Talk about spoilt.' Sandi grinned.

Mallory had opened the door before Sandi called, 'Oh, I forgot to tell you who was in here. The most dashingly handsome and gorgeous man I've ever seen in my life. He was really tall, about six feet four, I'd say, with the most wonderful thick black hair that I could just run my fingers through for ever and—'

'Hypnotic blue eyes,' Mallory finished. Her voice was a whisper and the dread she'd felt earlier rose up once again. 'Nicholas Sterling.'

'You know him?' Sandi's eyebrows rose to meet her fringe.

'You could say that.' Mallory shook her head dejectedly and sighed. 'Milk, no sugar—right?'

'Yeah, but, Mallory...'

Mallory didn't wait to be questioned by her receptionist. She stalked to the communal kitchen which was shared by the staff of the medical centre. Clive Bower, the local obstetrician, was sitting at the table with a smile on his face.

'What are you so happy for?' Mallory asked, trying to keep the anger from her voice. She and Clive had been friends for years and business colleagues for the past three. They'd had the initial idea of starting this medical centre, which offered many different specialties for the local community and surrounding districts.

'Ever since Jason left two years ago to practice in Brisbane, I've been searching to fill his place.'

'But I thought we agreed we didn't require the services of a general surgeon.' Mallory eyed him cautiously.

'I know, but this medical centre has a good range of specialities—dentistry, physiotherapy, marvellous obstetrician.' He straightened his tie with pride. 'Dietian, physician, paediatrician, a brilliant general practitioner.' Clive gave her a wink. 'And a general surgeon is an added bonus.'

'But not a bonus we need.' Her coffee forgotten, she sat down next to Clive. 'We're doing fine without one. Brisbane is less than an hour away by road—less by helicopter. If people need a general surgeon, they go to Brisbane. Why change status quo now?'

'I thought you'd be happy.' Clive gave her an intense look. 'What's the real problem, Mallory?'

'I'd say it's me.' The deep, resonant voice came from the doorway. Mallory didn't need to turn in her chair to see whom it belonged. She'd have recognised it anywhere. The spiral of desire shot through her and she once again cursed it. She had no idea how she could be attracted to a man she despised.

Rising to her feet, she knew the time had come to face him. Turning slowly, she physically unclenched her jaw and wrapped a mental shield around herself. The Sterling charm had been known to break through all barriers and she had vowed *never* to leave herself open to it again.

Their eyes met and held for a second. Sandi's description of him had been accurate. He was devastatingly handsome.

He was dressed in denim jeans and a white polo shirt. His hair was as dark as midnight, with a hint of grey at his temples.

'Mallory.' Nick gave her a nod. 'Good to see you again.'

Mallory glared. 'Of all the rotten qualities you possess, Nick, I never pegged you for a liar.' Considering his presence had once again shaken her foundations, she was happy to hear that her voice sounded calm and controlled.

'Fair enough,' he replied with a nonchalant shrug. 'It's not good to see you. Better?'

'Uh, without wanting to state the obvious, I gather you two know each other.' Clive rose from the table. 'Everything settled at the real estate office? Good,' Clive answered his own question, before beating a quick retreat and leaving them alone.

'Tactful man.' Nick lowered his tall frame into a chair.

'He's a wimp.' Mallory busied herself with the coffee.

'No. Definitely smart to get out of your firing line.'

'*He's* not in my firing line.'

Nick made a pretence of looking around the deserted room. 'I guess that only leaves me.'

'So why, Nick?' Mallory asked calmly, although she could feel the old familiar volcano begin to bubble deep down inside her. The volcano that held all her feelings—good and bad—toward Nick Sterling. 'Why are you here? Are you following me? Deliberately trying to ruin my peaceful life?'

'Of course I am, but then you wouldn't expect anything else, would you, Mallory?' He shrugged. 'And I wouldn't want to disappoint you.'

'Why spare my feelings now? You never bothered in the past.'

He clenched his jaw, before relaxing and allowing his lips to curve into a teasing smile. 'Bitterness, Mallory? Or perhaps...regrets?'

'Neither! Annoyance is more the word I would use to describe my feelings toward you. What's wrong with your thriving and lucrative practice in Brisbane? When I saw you six months ago at the retrieval team procedures you seemed relatively settled.'

'You only saw me for a couple of minutes so how could you come to such a conclusion?' When she remained silent he continued, 'There are many reasons for my move back to Appleton.' His eyes glinted with defiant humour. 'You are one of them. After I saw you in Brisbane it made me remember all that we'd shared. What we used to have together.'

'We had *nothing* together, Nick. You dumped me for my best friend when I was twenty-five. It means nothing now.'

'Now who's lying?' Nick raised his eyebrows in disbelief at her words.

'Oh, my,' she said with derision. 'The ego is still there and hasn't diminished one bit.'

Mallory crossed to the fridge to retrieve the milk. She could feel his eyes watching her every move. The subtle sway of her hips beneath the navy cotton skirt. The rigidness of her spine under the matching navy shirt.

With her back still to him, she asked, 'What are the other reasons? Is Kate one of them?' She collected two cups and spooned in some instant coffee. The actions were automatic but, after putting three sugars into her own cup when she usually only had one, she knew she wasn't concentrating on anything but Nick's response.

'Kate?' His voice sounded puzzled and she risked a glance over her shoulder to read his expression. His forehead was furrowed in a frown, as though he was trying to recall who Kate was.

Mallory felt herself relax. If he couldn't remember who Kate was, surely that was a good sign. Although she didn't know why the thought of Nick and Kate together bothered her so much.

'Ah yes. Kate. The lovely blonde nurse who was part of the retrieval team. Now, why would you ask about her, Mal?'

Mallory kept her back to him. 'Well…she told me that the two of you had really hit it off when you all to dinner that night.'

'Did she now? We did have a good night. Why do you ask, Mal?'

Mallory's spine stiffened as she heard him get out of the chair and come to stand behind her.

'You're not…*jealous*, are you?' His voice was almost a whisper and his breath fanned her neck. She could feel her body respond to his closeness, even though he wasn't touching her. Mallory closed her eyes and tried to control not only her breathing but her wayward emotions as well.

'Jealous?' Her voice cracked on the word and she cleared her throat. 'Why would I be jealous?'

'Why indeed.' He was silent for a moment. 'You've cut your hair,' he stated, his voice still soft. 'The last time I saw you it was almost down to your waist.'

'Changes do happen. It was highly unpractical for my internship.' She poured hot water from the urn into the cups and began to stir them.

'It looks good shoulder-length. More professional.'

Mallory fought against his deep, sensual tone. It washed over her like silk, making her feel vulnerable. Striving for self-preservation, Mallory knew she had to get out of the kitchen as quickly as possible. Lifting the coffee-cups, she tried to block out his words.

'I've always loved the colour. Rich, dark brown—to match your eyes.' He raised a hand and let his fingers slide through her hair.

Mallory sucked in her breath at the contact and jerked away from his touch. 'Ouch,' she wailed as hot coffee spilled over her hand. 'Now look what you've done,' she said crossly and slammed the cups back onto the bench. Her temper rising to the fore, she silently berated herself for falling prey to his charms once again.

Within an instant he'd grasped her hand and was holding it under cold, running water at the sink. 'Tut-tut-tut,' he said,

'Who are you? Skippy the kangaroo?' She attempted to jerk out of his hold.

He favoured her with a smile. 'When did you get so clumsy?'

'It's fine. Let me go.' She tried to pull her hand away but he only tightened his grip.

'Hold still or you'll blister,' he commanded.

Knowing he was right, Mallory conceded to his wishes. As the water cascaded over the pink tinge on her hand where the coffee had spilt, cooling and healing at the same time, a deeper burning took place around her wrist.

Nick's grip was firm but the touch of his flesh on hers was doing more damage and affecting her far worse than any scalding ever could. Mallory closed her eyes as she breathed in the scent of his aftershave. Her whole body seemed to be tingling with awareness of his close proximity. Although only his hand was touching her, she could feel the warmth his body exuded and it enveloped her like a glove.

'Mallory.' A female voice called from a distance.

Mallory's eyes snapped open. It was Sandi. 'Let me go.' She looked at Nick, demanding he free her hand.

'I knew she'd get sidetracked on the way to the kit—'

the receptionist was grumbling but, on reaching the doorway, stopped where she was. 'Oh, sorry. I didn't realise…'

Mallory watched Sandi's eyes rake over Nick's figure and a grin spread across her face at the horrified look on her employer's. '…I was interrupting anything.' She turned to leave, closing the door behind her.

'No. Wait. Sandi…' But Mallory was too late. The door was shut and Nick still hadn't let go of her hand.

'It's fine now.' She switched the tap off with her free hand, before trying again to push him away. His grip remained solid. 'Let me go,' she repeated.

He bent his head closer to hers and whispered 'What's the magic word, Mallory?'

Gritting her teeth, she hissed, 'Ple-eeze.'

'Say, ''Pretty please with a cherry on top.'''

'Nick!' Her eyes were clouded with rage at his audacity.

'Say it—or I'll be holding your hand for ever.'

She opened her mouth to speak but he held up a finger to silence her. 'And say it like you mean it.'

Mallory breathed in deeply, then slowly exhaled. 'Pretty please with a cherry on top,' she said, and hoped she'd kept the venom out of her voice.

'Pretty please with a cherry on top…what?'

'Oh, for heaven's sake, Nick. Just let go of my hand. You're beginning to hurt me.' She'd lost all patience with him—if she'd had any to begin with.

'If I do let go, will you stay and talk to me?'

'No. I'm expecting a patient and you've just completely ruined the only ten minutes I've had to myself all day.'

'Have dinner with me tonight. At my place.'

'No.'

'Why not?' His eyes narrowed slightly and the grip on her hand increased only by a fraction as he waited for her reply.

'I've got nothing to say to you.'

'Perhaps.' He shrugged. 'But I have plenty I'd like to say to you.'

'No doubt,' she mumbled, and he smiled, indicating he'd heard.

'Come on. I've just finished signing all the papers for my new home. My housekeeper, Arlene, has been here for the past week, setting things up all ready for my arrival.'

'Then you'll hardly want company.'

'Quite the contrary. Tonight will be a celebration of a new beginning. Arlene is a competent cook and will have a fabulous meal on the table—nutritionally balanced, of course.

'No. Thank you.' The last two words were said grudgingly. Mallory realised she'd have to play it carefully if she was going to get to her clinic on time, without having to scream the place down for assistance in getting Nick to let her go.

'Your manners are improving dramatically but I won't take no for an answer.'

'What will you take?'

His eyes flashed with desire but thankfully he decided to ignore the *double entendre*. 'Only an affirmative reply.'

'Nick!' Mallory's exasperation began to grow. 'I have other plans for tonight, not to mention a busy Friday afternoon clinic to get through. Who knows what time I'll be finished?'

'I can just imagined what your "plans" consist of. Probably a microwave dinner with a medical text.'

At the sheepish look in her eyes he nodded. 'I'm right.' He shook his head. 'You leave me no option but to play my trump card.'

Mallory tried hard to make her expression appear bored with the whole conversation but secretly she was curious to hear what it was.

'You'll get to meet Rebekah.' The words were spoken softly and Nick knew they'd served their purpose.

Her hand forgotten, Mallory looked at him with amazement. 'She's here? You...you have her?'

'I most certainly do. After all, she is my daughter. Rebekah Mallory Sterling—your namesake.'

He had never played fair. As long as she'd known him, he'd been able to manipulate situations and people to get exactly what he wanted, and he'd played just the right card with her. She was desperate to see his daughter.

'How old is she now?'

'As if you have to ask. I know you and Suzannah kept in contact. Rebekah is two-and-a-half years old and quite a handful at times.' He smiled as memories of his daughter intruded. 'So, shall we expect you, say, around seven-ish? If you like, you can bath her. She's very generous with her cuddles.'

Pain and anguish twisted deep within Mallory at the picture painted for her. To be able to bath her best friend's daughter. To touch, hold and cuddle Suzannah's little girl. The thoughts were all too much.

Nick raised her hand to his lips and, after releasing his grip, tenderly kissed first the slightly pink flesh where the coffee had scalded her and then where his fingers and thumb had pressed into her.

Then he placed a hand under her chin, lifting her head to meet his gaze.

'This is a new beginning, Mallory.' He bent his head and settled a brief kiss on her waiting lips. Mallory closed her eyes and savoured the short caress. Her heart was pounding against her chest and she was sure he could hear it. Her knees were almost about to give way and she swayed slightly as he let her go.

'I'll see you tonight.'

Mallory didn't move until she'd heard the door open and

close, then she slumped into the nearest chair and buried her face in her hands. As sanity began to return, contempt rose within her for allowing him to touch her in such an intimate manner, especially when she hadn't retaliated. She should have slapped his face for treating her in such a way.

Who did he think he was? He'd been married to Suzannah for three years, and two years after her death he was fooling around with her friend. Not that he'd been faithful during his marriage. The few times Suzannah had returned to Appleton for a visit, Nick had always been overseas at conferences.

She'd confided to Mallory that she'd suspected Nick of having affairs but as she'd loved him dearly, she'd always forgiven him. As Nick had two-timed Mallory with Suzannah, it had come as no real surprise. He'd also been very busy with his practice which had left little time for his wife.

Appearances had been kept in place and no one, except Mallory, had known of Nick's deceit and unfaithfulness to his wife. After being forced to be bridesmaid at their wedding, purely for Suzannah's sake, Mallory had vowed never to see or have anything to do with Nick Sterling again.

She'd judged it unwise to attend Suzannah's funeral for fear she'd tell Nick exactly what she'd thought of him. If he'd stopped to spend a bit more time with his wife and attended to her needs, especially her emotional needs, then perhaps Suzannah would be alive today.

Oh, he had a nerve, striding into her life again as though the past five years hadn't happened. He'd known that, by using little Rebekah as bait, she'd jump at the chance to meet the little girl Suzannah had begged her to be godmother to. Mallory had accepted the honour but had refused to attend the ceremony. As proxy, Suzannah had chosen another acquaintance who'd had no interest in children whatsoever.

Poor Rebekah. Only six months old when her mother had died in a terrible car accident, then left in the care of a housekeeper while her ambitious father had continued on his world tour, promoting his latest breakthrough in operating techniques.

Yes, Mallory had been surprised to learn he had custody of Rebekah rather than Suannah's parents but he *was* her father, even though Suzannah had often told her he had no interest in the baby. The one time Mallory had seen Rebekah had been when she'd been only eight weeks old. Suzannah had returned to Appleton for her annual visit. Mallory had been swamped at the clinic and had been unable to spend a lot of time with the baby—as much as she'd have chosen otherwise.

Suzannah had bottle-fed the baby, stating that her milk had dried up immediately, yet not once during her visit had she allowed Mallory to give Rebekah a bottle. Suzannah had insisted on doing it herself every time, saying it brought her closer to the little darling.

Rebekah had slept well through the first two nights but on the third night Suzannah had been hard pressed to calm her down. When Mallory had offered help, she'd been brutally rebuffed, and early the next morning Suzannah and Rebekah had returned to Brisbane.

Suzannah had said some horrible things to Mallory but two weeks later had phoned to apologise. That had been the only time Mallory had seen Rebekah as four months later Suzannah had died.

Now Nick was offering an olive branch—where his daughter was concerned. It had certainly been an effective measure dousing her own anger towards him. The maternal emptiness inside her ached to be filled and she knew, as did Nick, that she could not have kept away from the child who so desperately needed a mother's love—even if it was just a godmother's love.

Mallory glanced down at her watch and realised the ten minutes were well and truly up. She would make sure she finished as close to time as possible. Dining with Nick would hold no pleasure but the chance to finally hold Rebekah Mallory was something she'd only dreamed about.

# CHAPTER TWO

MRS KOOS was hidden behind a magazine and Sandi had an inquisitive look on her face. Recalling the scene the receptionist had witnessed, Mallory coloured.

'Here's your coffee.'

'Thanks.' Sandi accepted the cup, then frowned at the lukewarm temperature. 'Perhaps we should leave the coffee-making to me. Who knows? It seems like a good way to catch yourself a handsome stranger.'

Mallory opened her mouth to say something but closed it again. Trying to explain her relationship—no, she corrected herself, her *acquaintance* with Nick Sterling—was too complex...and too hurtful.

'Give me a few seconds to get ready, before sending Mrs Koos in.' Mallory carried her cup through to her office and sat down. Then she noticed the bowl of melted fudge ice cream, still sitting on the desk. 'Damn you, Nick Sterling.' She took a sip of her coffee and agreed with Sandi's assessment. 'Damn you,' she repeated.

Not about to waste her ice cream, she buzzed for Sandi to come through. 'Could you put this into the freezer for me? I'll get it later.'

'Sure thing. Stuart Dellingham has just arrived.'

At this announcement Mallory realised she was indeed going to be running late. 'Thanks. Send Mrs Koos through.'

'I'm sorry to have kept you waiting, Mrs Koos,' Mallory apologised a few moments later as her patient sat down. 'What can I help you with today?'

'Well, dear...' Mrs Koos looked down at her hands,

which were clasped tightly together. 'I've been feeling a bit…under the weather.'

Mallory nodded. 'It's been a few months since you had a general check-up and from my notes everything seemed fine then.' Mallory paused for a moment, keeping her voice gentle. 'In what way don't you feel well?'

Mrs Koos seemed to be fighting something deep inside and after a few awkward seconds blurted out, 'I've been vomiting.'

'How often?'

'Almost every morning. I'm pregnant, aren't I?' The worried look on her face told Mallory that the possibility had been eating away at her for quite some time.

'When was your last period?'

'At least three to four weeks ago. Oh, dear, I just know I'm pregnant.'

'It's all right, Mrs Koos,' Mallory soothed. 'Have you been having hot flushes? Problems sleeping at night or night sweats?'

Mrs Koos thought for a moment. 'Yes. Now that you mention it, I have, but I put it down to worry about this pregnancy.'

Mallory consulted her notes. 'You're now forty-seven, is that correct?'

'Yes.'

'It is possible that you're beginning the menopause.' Mallory stood and went to her cupboard. She took out a sample container. 'First of all, why don't we address the pregnancy query. If you could provide me with a urine sample, I'll do the test immediately.'

'Thank you,' Mrs Koos said as she reached out a shaky hand for the container.

'You can go through this door.' Mallory held open a side door which was directly opposite the bathroom. Once Mrs Koos had gone, Mallory collected the pregnancy test kit and set things up. Putting on a pair of gloves, she waited for her patient's return.

'Do you really think it is the menopause?' Mrs Koos asked hopefully as she walked back into the room.

'It's certainly possible.' Mallory took the container and motioned for Mrs Koos to sit down while she performed the test.

'But I thought the change of life wasn't supposed to come until I was in my fifties.'

'It can come as early as forty—it all depends on the individual.' Mallory looked down at the test, waiting for the result. She turned and smiled at Mrs Koos. 'It's negative. You're not pregnant.'

Relief washed over the other woman's face as she visibly relaxed in the chair. 'Jonathan wouldn't have been happy if I had been.'

'Have you discussed the situation with him?'

'No. Oh, no.' She shook her head emphatically.

'What about the vomiting? Didn't he realise you were sick most mornings?'

'No. He leaves for work very early.'

'You have two sons, don't you?'

'Yes. Both of them live and work in Brisbane.' A smile had lit her face at the mention of her sons.

'How old are they?' Mallory wanted Mrs Koos to relax a bit more before they went on with the examination.

'Gideon is twenty-four and Harold is twenty-two. They love their jobs, and when I spoke with Gideon last night he told me he's met a wonderful woman. He's going to bring her home to meet us soon so I think it might be serious.'

'You'd like to see them married, wouldn't you?'

'It's every mother's dream. Then I can get on with being a grandmother.'

Mallory smiled at the transformation in her patient. 'That would be wonderful.'

'I kept thinking I was pregnant and how it was so late in life for us to have another child, and then when I thought of my son settling down and having children of his own…well, I guess I let my imagination get carried away. It was silly of me.'

'It was nothing of the kind. Until a woman has gone through menopause she's still quite fertile and should practise safe sex.'

'You mean I could still get pregnant?'

'While you're still ovulating, yes, but we know that you're not currently pregnant and are exhibiting symptoms of menopause. Let's go from there and do what we can to make things a bit more comfortable for you.'

Mallory discussed several relaxation techniques to help at night with the insomnia and how to relieve the night sweats and hot flushes.

'As I said before, every woman's experience is different. Some go through menopause with little distress while others need a little more help. There are many natural herbal remedies to assist the process. In your case I suggest we take things one step at a time.' Mallory wrote out a prescription. 'This is for the nausea you've been experiencing. I suspect that now your current worries have been alleviated you may not feel as sick in the mornings, but if the vomiting persists over the next few days I want you to come back and see me. Immediately.'

'I will, Dr Newman.' Mrs Koos stood, a happier woman than when she'd come in. 'Thank you so much.'

'My pleasure.' Mallory smiled to herself as she wrote up the notes on Mrs Koos. It made her feel so good, being able to help her patients. When she'd finished she pressed the buzzer for her next patient then consulted the clock on the wall.

She was definitely running late now, but she preferred to run late and devote her time to her patients rather than hustle them through.

Being late for dinner wasn't something she wanted as her desire to see Rebekah was growing by the second, but for the moment she pulled out Stuart Dellingham's card and waited for him to come through her door.


Pressing her finger to the doorbell, Mallory shifted the present for Rebekah to her other hand and smoothed down her top. Ridiculous, she chided herself. Being so preoccupied with her appearance simply for a toddler. This was the fourth outfit she'd changed into, before leaving home.

Thankfully, due to a cancellation, Mallory had been able to stop by the real estate office and obtain Nick's address as he hadn't thought to give it to her. Peter McPhee's eyes had sparkled momentarily but he'd held his tongue and simply given her the address, although she'd been able to tell his interest had definitely been piqued.

Next she had gone to the toy store. Long minutes of deliberation had resulted in her buying an animated clock which was guaranteed to lull any child to sleep and bring a giggle to their lips during the day.

Resisting the impulse to press the doorbell again, Mallory fluffed her ankle-length floral skirt and checked that her white top was tucked in at the waist. Where on earth was he? Why didn't he open the door?

She'd told herself over and over that she wasn't here to see Nick but to meet his darling daughter. Taking a step back, she looked up to a window on the upper floor where a light was shining out brightly into the August evening. They were definitely home.

After a few more impatient moments she heard footsteps, heading towards the door. Exhaling a deep breath, she pasted a smile in place.

'Dr Newman?' The door was opened by a plump, middle aged woman with short grey hair and green eyes.

'Yes,' Mallory said when she finally found her voice.

'Won't you come in, Dr Newman? Nick is expecting you.'

'Thank you. Please, call me Mallory.'

'As you wish.' She closed the door. 'I'm Arlene.' She glanced at the beautifully wrapped present and smiled. 'Rebekah is going to love that wrapping paper.'

Mallory laughed. 'Not to mention the box. I specifically chose the shiny paper for that very reason.'

Arlene gave her a quick nod and Mallory had the strangest feeling she'd just passed a test. 'Come this way.' She walked through the house, her flat shoes making a faint tapping sound on the polished wooden floor. 'We'll be eating straight away so Rebekah can have her bath and go bed.'

'Sounds good,' Mallory agreed. 'It's important to keep their routine, regardless of what happens around them.'

Arlene paused with her hand on a doorknob and gave Mallory another satisfied glance. 'Exactly.' She opened the door and waited for Mallory to precede her. The large dining table was set down at one end with four place settings— the fourth having a Micky Mouse theme. Place mat, fork, spoon and cup were all adorned with Disney character markings. A booster seat was on the chair and Nick, with his back to Mallory, was seating his daughter comfortably.

When he stepped away, Mallory's heart jumped into her throat and tears misted her eyes. Rebekah sat, her large blue eyes sparkling with happiness as she smiled up at her father. The blue eyes then focused on Mallory and after a faltering second Rebekah's face lit up with glee.

'Present!' she squealed with delight, and held out her hands for the parcel Mallory held.

'Yes, sweetheart.' Mallory walked towards the table and gave Rebekah the present. 'This is for you.'

The red bow was expertly pulled off the top and the sound of paper being torn filled the air. 'Pretty,' Rebekah said, and Mallory's heart constricted with love at the delight on the two-and-a-half-year-old's face.

She had a mop of short brown curls, rosy cheeks and pink lips. With the same blue eyes as her father, Rebekah Mallory Sterling was an exquisite looking child.

'You look lovely,' Nick said quietly.

Mallory turned her head and smiled apologetically. 'I'm sorry. I didn't mean to be so rude.'

He smiled warmly. 'It's perfectly all right. She tends to capture attention wherever she goes. I'm used to being passed over.' He looked down at his daughter, who had managed to get the ribbon off and was scrunching the shiny gold paper. 'Would you like some help, pumpkin?' He carefully removed the sticky tape and lifted the box out of her reach. The paper was what she was interested in and she was soon rustling and scrunching it up, enjoying the sound it made.

'Look what's in here, Becka.' Nick opened the box and took out the clock.

'Wow!' Rebekah exclaimed. 'Cow. Dog. Cat. 'Poon.'

'It's "Hey Diddle Diddle," Nick told her. Rebekah reached for the clock and her father quickly said, 'Gently, Becka. Touch them lightly.'

The clock, shaped like a moon, had three-dimensional characters from the nursery rhyme around it.

'It plays two different tunes,' Mallory volunteered. 'One for bedtime and one for daytime.' She'd put a battery in and set the clock to the correct time, before wrapping it. Nick sat it on the table, out of reach of little fingers, and flicked the button that controlled the music.

The strains of 'Hey Diddle Diddle' filled the room as the

cat fiddled, the cow jumped over the moon, the dog laughed
and a small dish and spoon moved across the base.
Rebekah's eyes grew wide and she clapped her hands when
it had finished.

'Again, Daddy. Again.'

Nick flicked the switch over to the night-time song and
soon the strains of Brahms' Lullaby filled the room.
Rebekah clapped her hands again. Although the characters
continued to move in the same way, the music was softer
and more peaceful. Nick yawned and stretched and Mallory
laughed again. She'd forgotten how much fun he could be.

'It definitely works for Daddy,' he told Rebekah with a
grin, then tickled his daughter. 'Thanks, Mal. It's a wonderful gift.'

'My pleasure.' Their eyes held for a moment. Both
seemed to be remembering happier times, times they'd
shared.

When the music began for the third time, Nick groaned
and switched it off.

'More, please. More, Daddy.'

'Later. It's time for dinner now. Say, "thank you, Mal."'

'Dank you, Mal,' Rebekah said dutifully.

'You're welcome,' Mallory replied.

'I presume both tunes are continuous play?' Nick asked.
When Mallory nodded he groaned.

'And I made sure I put long-life batteries in.'

'How considerate,' he teased, and rolled his eyes.

'Sorry for the slight delay.' Arlene came through the
swinging door from the kitchen. She carried a tray with
their steaming meals. Placing them on the table, she said,
'Sit down before it gets cold.' She eyed the empty wine-
glasses and tut-tutted at Nick. 'Do I have to do everything?'

Nick smiled and reached for the bottle of white wine that
stood, chilling, in a silver bucket. He wiped the base and

began to pour. 'You *are* the hired help,' Nick pointed out as Arlene sat down.

'That's what he tells everyone,' Arlene replied, placing a serviette in her lap. 'Just because he pays me a salary he expects me to be his slave.'

Mallory looked from one to the other before she realised they were comfortable with the conversation. Nick caught her look as he sat down.

'Don't worry, Mallory. We're only joking. Arlene has been my housekeeper since I first moved to Brisbane five years ago. Before that she was employed by my grandfather. When he died I felt sorry for her so I offered her a job.'

Arlene waggled a finger at him. 'You're not too old for me to put you over my knee, Nicholas Sterling.'

'She's known me since I was born so there's absolutely nothing I can get away with.' Nick unfolded his serviette then secured the bib around Rebekah's neck.

'Let's say grace,' Arlene instructed. At the word 'grace' Rebekah held out her hands and Mallory took one with delight.

She soon found her other hand encompassed firmly in Nick's. His fingers tightened and she glanced at him, but his head was bent as he concentrated on Arlene's words.

'Ah-men,' Rebekah said emphatically when Arlene was finished. Then she quickly withdrew her hand and picked up her spoon. Mallory watched as the child began to feed herself, chasing the food around on her Micky Mouse plate before successfully collecting it up onto her spoon and into her mouth.

Mallory went to pick up her own fork but found her hand once again captured in Nick's.

'Thanks for coming,' he said sincerely, and gave her fingers a squeeze, before releasing them. 'At least now that Rebekah can feed herself we generally get to eat our own

meals hot. Gone are the days of lukewarm dinners.'
Without further hesitation he started eating his food.

Conversation for the next half-hour was about general
topics. Nick had told Mallory he had a few things to say
to her and she was almost dreading being alone with him.
What was he going to say? She knew he could sense her
automatic response to him—even though she was still desperately trying to deny it.

The tension, the anticipation, the desire and the passion
were all simmering below the surface and Mallory wondered how much longer she could retain her self-control.
She risked a glance at him as he replied to something
Arlene had asked. He was a most handsome man. The lines
around his eyes creased upwards as a warm smile lit up his
face, his eyes twinkling with amusement. Nick was fasci-
nating, charming and funny, but he was also opinionated,
arrogant and extremely ruthless—and it would do her good
to remember that.

He turned his head and looked at her, the smile still
lighting his face. Rebekah dropped her fork on the floor
and he quickly bent to retrieve it.

'There you are, funny face.'

Rebekah giggled and blew a kiss to her beloved daddy.
Mallory was completely captivated by their relationship.
Suzannah had told her that Nick had had no interest in their
baby, but to see the two of them together now it was obvious that they loved each other very deeply. Perhaps…
perhaps Nick had changed in the two years since his wife's
death.

Rebekah was delightful. In less than an hour she had
managed to nestle her way right into the centre of Mallory's
heart. Knowing she could never have children of her own,
it made her time with Rebekah more precious yet more
heartbreaking.

Tears welled in her eyes and she impatiently brushed

them away before she glanced up at Nick to find him studying her with a puzzled expression. Mallory gave him a brief
smile, before turning her attention back to her meal.

Remembering her manners, and in an effort to school her
thoughts, Mallory praised Arlene's cooking.

'Better than a microwave dinner?' Nick queried.

'Most definitely,' she agreed readily.

'Don't tell me you eat those cardboard meals?' Arlene
was obviously quite surprised.

Mallory opened her mouth to explain but Nick did it for
her.

'Although the medical centre sports quite a number of
medical professionals, Mallory is the only general practitioner. Therefore, she has the highest intake of patients and
is on call twenty-four hours per day, seven days per week,
three hundred and sixty-five days per year. I doubt, Arlene,
that cooking meals is high on her busy agenda.'

'But surely the hospital takes some of the pressure off
you?'

'Yes and no,' Mallory responded. 'Country folk don't
find it easy to break their lifelong habits. Most people still
prefer to see their doctor privately, rather than turn up at
the hospital's casualty department. I guess it makes them
feel less like a unit record number and more like a person.
I have quite a lot to do with the hospital.'

'Do you mean you don't have a housekeeper?' Arlene
asked, quite appalled at the prospect. 'Someone to clean
your place and prepare a wholesome, home-cooked meal
for you daily?'

'I'm afraid not.'

'Mallory's a very neat person,' Nick commented, and
received a raised eyebrow from Arlene as if asking how he
knew such an intimate thing.

'We've known each other for…quite a while,' he said

matter-of-factly. 'Her brother Jeff is one of my closest
friends. We went through school together.'

A look of dawning realisation crossed Arlene's face.
'Jeff Newman. The paediatrician. Of course. I can see a
slight resemblance, now that you mention it.'

Mallory's smile came easily at the mention of her
brother. 'Have you spoken to him lately?'

'Unfortunately, no. Since his last move to Townsville,
I've not caught up with him.'

'He's doing well and enjoying himself,' Mallory reported.

'Good to hear.'

At a loud crash, they all re-focused their attention on
Rebekah, who had managed to knock her plate onto the
floor. She looked dubiously at her father and then Arlene
before her eyes went back to her father.

'Oops-a-daisy,' Nick said, and placed it back on the table. Rebekah's smile returned when she realised she wasn't
in trouble.

'Sorwwy, Daddy,' she said with an angelic smile on her
face.

'Have you finished?' Arlene asked.

'Yes. Weave table, peeze?'

'Yes, you may leave the table,' Nick answered, and
helped his daughter out of her chair.

'Becka go play,' she announced and ran from the room.
They could hear her footsteps as she climbed the stairs and
then trotted down the hallway.

'She'll play in her room for about ten minutes before
bathtime,' Nick told Mallory.

'Routine is very important in their little lives,' Mallory
responded. 'I remember my mother telling me that the ''terrible twos'', as some people term them, aren't terrible at
all. It's just the child pushing its boundaries to discover

what it's capable of. But it's the parents' responsibility to set the outer limits of those boundaries.'

'Your mother sounds like a very sensible woman,' Arlene nodded.

'She is.'

'Does she live here in Appleton?' Arlene asked as she began clearing the table.

'No. She returned to England six months ago. My father died just before I finished my final year of GP training three years ago. As Mum had come to Australia to be with him, now that he'd gone she decided to return home to be back with the rest of her family.'

'That doesn't bother you?' Arlene asked.

'I miss her, desperately, but once I started working in the practice I was hardly home. I used to worry about her, so this way I know she's happy.'

'I remember Jeff telling me you took over your father's practice,' Nick recalled with a hint of admiration in his voice. 'Quite large footsteps you had to follow in, Mal.'

Mallory smiled. 'Large? More like ginormous footsteps.'

'I always held him in the highest esteem. I was sorry to hear of his death.' Nick's words comforted Mallory like a warm blanket.

'Thank you. It means a lot to hear you say that.'

'If you'll excuse me,' Arlene interrupted, 'I'll go run the bath and check on the little mosquito.'

'Mosquito?' Mallory asked after Arlene had left them alone.

'One of Arlene's sayings is that children are like mosquitoes. When they stop buzzing you know they're into something.'

Mallory laughed. 'So true.' She stretched. 'I'm so full. The meal was delicious but very filling.'

'Arlene probably thinks you're too thin and need a little more flesh on your bones.' Nick stood and walked to the window. 'She's right. You've lost quite a bit of weight and I can see the strain of an overworked doctor in your eyes.'

'Come off it, Nick.' Mallory stood and crossed to the window beside him. 'It's been years since you last saw me. I was plump back then and just starting my internship.'

'Yes. I've always been amazed at how you managed to transfer your internship training from Brisbane to Sydney so quickly. I presume your father pulled a few strings for you?'

When Mallory didn't answer, merely looking at him with a bland expression on her face, he nodded. She guessed he knew she'd done it to get as far away from him as possible. She hadn't wanted to run the risk of meeting him around the hospital so she'd completed her internship and most of her GP rotation in Sydney.

'Besides,' Nick continued, 'if my memory serves me correctly, you were never "plump" The main difference between that twenty-five-year-old woman and the person who stands beside me is happiness. You're not as happy as you were back then, Mal. What happened?'

Mallory looked down at her hands, then back out the window. She wasn't game enough to look him in the eye. Emotions she'd rather have forgotten began to re-emerge now that Nick had come back into her life.

'As if you need to ask.' Her voice was a whisper, as though the words were extremely hard for her to admit.

He was silent, before saying quietly, 'Things happened very fast back then. Believe me, if I could have spared you the pain I would have.'

Attempting to toughen up, she said firmly, 'Don't lose any sleep over it, Nick. I got over the pain and put my life in perspective. When you dumped me for Suzannah you did me a big favour. You helped me to grow up—overnight—from a gullible woman into a strong woman who hasn't let herself be taken advantage of since.'

'I didn't dump you, Mal.'

She glanced up at him. 'Oh, no?' Anger at his audacity began to rise throughout her being. 'Perhaps two-timing swine is a better description. After all, one day you and I were talking about getting engaged and the next thing I knew you were engaged to Suzannah instead.' Mallory turned and walked away from the window, putting some distance between them. 'My best friend, Nick. How could you?'

'She trapped me,' he argued as he turned to face her. 'I'm a man who lives up to his responsibilities.'

'Are you trying to blame her?' Mallory asked incredulously. 'That's a bit lame. She's dead, Nick. Suzannah can't even defend herself against your accusations but you needn't worry about that. She told me everything.'

'I'll just bet she did,' he growled. 'Suzannah's glorious imagination was working in overdrive as she twisted the truth to suit her purpose. Did she tell you she was pregnant? That she claimed it was my child?'

'How could you not believe her? She said you were both drunk and that she woke up in your arms. The next thing she knew she was pregnant. As you were the only person she'd slept with, there was no doubt of the parentage.'

Nick raked a hand through his hair. 'I always knew she was a low-life but I didn't expect that of her. I guess I should have known better.'

'How dare you talk about her like that?'

'You don't know the half of it, Mal.'

'Oh, no?' she challenged. 'Why don't you tell me?'

'Because it's quite obvious that anything I might say about Suzannah will be defended and discarded as lies.'

'She made no secret that your marriage wasn't a happy one, especially when she lost the baby on your honeymoon.'

'Oh, I'd almost forgotten about *that* one. I guess she told you I had no sympathy for her?'

'As a matter of fact, she did.'

'Figures.'

'What's that supposed to mean?'

'Forget it, Mallory. There's no point in discussing the truth of my relationship with Suzannah because you're not ready to acknowledge it as the truth.'

Mallory shook her head in disgust. 'Everything she told me was said with the utmost conviction and—'

'I'll bet it was,' he snarled. He continued to gaze into the blackness of the night. 'Why didn't you ever come to Brisbane to see her?' His voice was still firm but had lost its sniping tone.

'I came close a few times, especially when I was in Brisbane for conferences and meetings, but Suzannah always advised against it. Besides…' she trailed off, and Nick spun around to face her.

'Besides, what?'

When she stayed silent he crossed to stand in front of her. He lifted her chin so that their eyes met. 'It was me, wasn't it? You didn't want to see me.'

'Yes.' The confession came out as a whisper and Mallory felt her heart hammer in her chest.

'Because you still cared for me?'

'Cared for you. Hated you. Loved you. Despised you.' She pulled herself out of his grasp but his hands clamped around her arms, making sure she faced him. 'All of the above.'

'And now?'

Mallory swallowed, trying to control her accelerating pulse. 'Let me go, Nick.' She lowered her eyes and found herself hauled against him, enveloped in his arms. Being honest with herself, she acknowledged that she *didn't* want him to let her go.

'Not this time, Mallory.'

Despite his simmering anger, Nick's lips were gentle as they pressed against hers. It was a questioning kiss. Testing the waters. He pulled back slightly to look down into her eyes—gauge her reaction—and when he read the burning need for more of his touch he complied.

With ardent desire Mallory leaned closer to Nick, remembering with a rush how it felt to be held this way. In *his* arms, with *his* lips on hers.

Through the years Mallory had tried hard to bury the memory of Nick's kisses, but in her dreams they had always been fresh and realistic. Many a morning she'd woken, desperate for his touch, only to remember that he was married to Suzannah.

At this moment, Mallory didn't care what had happened in the past or what would happen in the future. All that mattered was the here and now—Nick's mouth on hers, his evident craving for her touch, the sexual attraction which had only strengthened over the passage of time.

His lips became more insistent, his appetite more demanding, and Mallory acquiesced, urging him on. His tongue delved deep into the sweetness of her mouth, meshing with her own as the fire within started to burn out of control.

This was where she belonged, Mallory thought through the haze of passion. She was his. She always had been... and always would...

'Rebekah's impatient to have her bath,' Arlene advised as she opened the door, releasing the naked little girl into the room.

Mallory instantly jumped out of Nick's arms, pushing him away as though burnt by his touch. She shivered slightly at the loss of his warmth, before raising her eyes shyly to meet his. He smiled at her and shrugged.

'Life with children,' he whispered. 'Always being interrupted.' His smile belied his words and Mallory watched as he scooped his daughter up, planting kisses and blowing raspberries on her abdomen.

Mallory tried to calm her wayward emotions. Why on earth had she allowed Nick to kiss her? What had she been thinking? Now he would know she was his for the taking. Deep breaths, she told herself. Slow down and focus on Rebekah. *She's* the reason you're here.

Rebekah squealed with delight as her father continued to tickle her. The child's infectious laughter filled the room with vibrance and colour, as well as causing the adults in the room to smile, the awkward moment broken.

'Stop it, Daddy,' she ordered between giggles, not meaning a word she said. Nick repeated the action, the sound of his lips on her stomach echoing around the room as Rebekah's laughter bubbled over.

'Is it bathtime already?' Nick asked his daughter.

'Yay, bathtime.' Rebekah clapped her hands.

'Ready to get drenched?' Nick asked Mallory as Arlene led the procession upstairs to the bathroom.

The bathtub had been filled with a generous amount of water and was covered with foaming masses of white bubbles. Once immersed, Rebekah searched for her toys amongst the bubbles, enjoying the game which was obviously a nightly ritual. She pulled out cups and boats and animals, delighting in each find.

The two adults stood side by side, watching the child play.

'She's gorgeous, Nick. Such a happy child.'

'You sound surprised.'

'Well…she has had a few upheavals in her young life.'

'All of which I hope she's already forgotten. Her memory span is roughly six to eight months at the moment so it should be only happy times she recalls.' His tone was calm yet defensive.

Mallory looked up at him apologetically. 'I didn't mean to criticise.'

Nick held her gaze, then smiled. 'No, I'm sure you didn't. Rebekah means the world to me, Mallory. She always has. Suzannah told me she was pregnant when I was three months into a year-long visiting professorship overseas. She was sixteen weeks along so I continued with my tour, receiving updates from her specialist after every appointment. When he advised me to come back I did—to be there for the birth of my child.

'You know how these visiting professorships are organised. My entire agenda for twelve months was meticulously planned, so taking time off wasn't easy. I still had just over four months to go after Rebekah's birth and had no option but to complete them.

'Two months after my return Suzannah was killed in the car accident. Arlene and I have been her family. I've cut my workload in half so we have more time together. It was one of the major reasons for the move back to Appleton. I loved growing up here in such a small community atmosphere, and I know it's the best thing for Rebekah.'

Mallory watched Rebekah as she played contentedly while she herself was listening to Nick. His version of Suzannah's pregnancy was completely different from the one she'd been told. Suzannah had called her weekly, sobbing that her husband refused to return from his overseas tour to be by her side.

Mallory had had no idea Nick had been chosen for a visiting professorship. There were only two such positions available per year for the entire world of medicine, and to be selected from all the finest surgeons around the globe was indeed an esteemed honour. No wonder Nick hadn't been able to return.

She didn't doubt Nick's side of the story as she could quite easily check up on the facts, therefore giving him no

reason to lie. It also rang true that he'd moved back to
Appleton for his daughter's sake. The community did look
after its own and, although it had expanded considerably
since Nick and Suzannah had left, the people were still very
close knit.

'Rebekah will make close friends, have people watching
out for her, caring about her. It will make a vast difference
to her life,' Nick continued. 'Besides all that, she'll have
you.'

'Me?' Mallory turned her head sharply to look at him.

His eyes were so intense that they mesmerised her. 'You
are planning on spending time with her, aren't you?'

'Do you want me to?'

'Most definitely, but I don't want her to become attached
to you only to have you disappear from her life.'

'What are you saying, Nick?'

'I don't want our past differences to get in the way of
you forming a relationship with my daughter. You love her,
Mallory. That much is evident and she needs a stable female figure in her life.'

'What about Arlene?'

'Arlene is more than a grandmother to her than her own
biological grandmother. As my parents are dead and
Suzannah's parents have no interest in Rebekah, she's for-
tunate to have Arlene to fill that void. What she also needs
is a mother figure, someone close to Suzannah's age.'

'Me,' she whispered, her eyes glued to the child playing
happily, unaware of the tension between them.

'If I recall correctly, you were only a few days older than
Suzannah. You were always mistaken for twin sisters because you looked so much alike. But age and appearances
are beside the point. You care for my daughter so naturally,
as though she were your own. That's special. Too special
to allow our differences to stand in the way.'

He reached out a hand and ran his fingers through her

hair. 'I know we have many unresolved issues and, I promise you, they *will* be resolved in the not too distant future, but for Rebekah's sake we should call a truce. She needs you—and you need her.' He rested his hand on her shoulder and she slowly turned her face to meet his hypnotic gaze.

'Spend as much time with her as you wish. My house is open to you at any time and I'm sure Arlene would welcome your company. My housekeeper is quite taken with you which, considering she doesn't like many people, is a very big compliment.

'Your busy schedule does allow for a few hours off here and there so consider spending them with Rebekah. I know it's what you want and I also know you'd never ask. You'd think you were imposing, which is why I wanted to say what I have.'

'And as usual,' Mallory said, swallowing over the lump in her throat, 'you won't take no for an answer.'

He smiled. 'See how well you know me!'

Rebekah reached out a hand to her father as both Mallory and Nick crouched down beside the bathtub. Rebekah then had great delight in bringing her hand down firmly onto the surface of the water. Splash! With one single motion they were thoroughly wet. They both laughed, which made Rebekah think she could do it again.

'Funny.' She giggled, before splashing once more.

'I think that's enough, scallywag.' Mallory grinned as she reached for the facecloth. 'Let's get you squeaky clean, then you can have another little play, before getting out.' She focused her attention on washing and playing with Rebekah.

Nick stood and resumed his position in the doorway, just watching the two of them together. He marvelled at how natural Mallory was with his daughter, while Suzannah had been cold and distant from the beginning.

He thought back to his comment about the resemblance

she bore to his wife. It was true. The two women had looked strikingly similar, but where Suzannah had gone for the glitz and glamour, Mallory had preferred to let her natural beauty shine from within.

If they were to meet a new acquaintance tomorrow, there would be no doubt that the child who sat before him, giggling in the bath and splashing water everywhere, was the daughter of the woman who sat beside her. The likeness was incredible.

She'd probably find it difficult to believe he still found her attractive. He always had and always would. Her hair looked more feminine cut to the shorter length and bouncing around her shoulders.

Nick knew some of his high-school friends had thought Mallory plain but he'd always been captivated, even when she'd been a teenager, by the combination of her dark brown hair and chocolaty-brown eyes.

Whoever had said that the eyes were the windows to the soul could have had Mallory Newman in mind. They were so deep with emotion that if he looked into them for too long he knew he'd drown. Suzannah, on the other hand, had never had the depth—of feeling or character—that Mallory had been born with.

Bitterness welled up from his gut. Suzannah had kept them apart for far too long with her lies. Now, though, it was imperative that Mallory learned the truth. The only factor he hadn't banked on five years ago had been that Mallory would choose to believe Suzannah rather than him.

They'd been close—in love—yet at the first sign of difficulty, she'd turned away from him, unwilling to even give him a chance to explain. Sure, Suzannah had fed him lies as well, telling him that Mallory had been having an affair with another colleague, but at least he'd checked them out and discovered the truth.

Yet Mallory had believed every word Suzannah had spouted, not once giving him the benefit of the doubt.

He watched the way she scooped his daughter carefully out of the bath and wrapped her in the waiting towel, before drawing Rebekah closer.

'Cuddle this little girl dry.' She wriggled Rebekah from side to side, making the child laugh. The sound was music to her heart. 'Come on, let's get you to your room and dressed for bed.'

Arlene was ready and waiting to take over. Rebekah's arms went out to her and she smiled gleefully.

Mallory watched as Arlene quickly dried and dressed the wriggling toddler, amazed at the other woman's speed at performing the task.

'Give Daddy a kiss goodnight,' Arlene instructed, and Rebekah instantly puckered her little lips up for her father. 'And a cuddle and kiss for Mallory.' That was Arlene's next order.

Rebekah eyed Mallory briefly, before holding out her arms for a cuddle. A lump caught in Mallory's throat as she held the child tenderly, closing her eyes to savour the moment. A kiss was placed on her cheek, then Rebekah marched back into the bathroom, claiming, 'Teef time.' She waited patiently for Arlene to hand her the toothbrush.

'Goodnight, darling.' Nick kissed her again and motioned for Mallory to leave.

'Don't you usually put her to bed?' Mallory asked as they walked downstairs.

'Usually but tonight, considering you're here, Arlene will do it.'

'Please,' Mallory implored. 'I don't want to disrupt the routine. You go back on up and I'll let myself out.'

'Just like that—you're leaving?' He quirked an eyebrow at her.

Mallory shrugged and looked down at her hands. 'I think I should.'

'No coffee? Arlene's prepared some. It's in the sitting room.' He pointed to a door at the end of the hallway. 'One cup, then I'll let you leave.'

She could tell he was teasing from the tone of his voice and she smiled. 'So kind of you, sir.' She accepted with a small curtsy.

'I knew you'd think so.' He led the way into the room. Boxes were pushed into the far corner but a Persian rug, comfortable lounge and coffee-table had been positioned for immediate use.

'Please, excuse the mess, but I know Arlene has been concentrating on getting Rebekah's room and the kitchen organised as first priorities. This room is way down the list.'

'Don't apologise,' Mallory said.

Arlene had certainly been busy as the small wooden table held a plate of biscuits, two cups, milk and sugar, not to mention a coffee-pot that filled the room with its delicious aroma.

As she sat down Mallory heard the sound she'd hoped not to hear throughout the night—the ringing of her mobile phone.

She looked across at Nick as she dug the phone out of her handbag and shrugged.

'You did well to get this far,' he commented.

She nodded in agreement, before connecting the call and saying, 'Dr Newman.'

Mallory listened while Nick poured her a cup of coffee and nodded when he pointed to the milk. When he motioned to the sugar she held up her index finger. Nick spooned in one sugar and stirred it, ready for her to drink.

'I see. Yes, Arthur. I'll be there in five minutes. Have a bag packed as she may need hospitalisation.' With that she concluded the call and picked up the coffee cup. Taking a few quick sips, she put it back on the table and stood.

'I have to go.'

'I understand.' He gave her a brisk nod.

'I'm afraid you don't, Mr Sterling. I need you to come with me.'

# CHAPTER THREE

'How old is Rose?' Nick asked as Mallory drove towards her patient's house. He'd uncomplainingly climbed into the front seat of her yellow Holden Barina, although she could sense he'd rather have been in the Jaguar XJ 6 she'd seen parked in the driveway.

'She's just turned sixty-two. She's been to see me previously for gallstone-related pain and has made a concentrated effort to cut back on her fatty food intake.'

'Is she considerably overweight?'

'About five to eight kilograms, but she's already lost five so she's doing well. I had hoped the pain would settle but obviously it hasn't.'

'I presume she's on analgesics for any painful attacks?'

'Yes. She's taken some.'

'Has she been reviewed by a general surgeon?'

'No. She was scheduled to see me in another two months when we were going to discuss things further, but it seems as though the gallstones have other ideas.' Mallory slowed the car and turned into a driveway. Every light in the house was on and, after parking, she and Nick moved quickly up the front steps.

'Arthur?' Mallory called as she knocked loudly on the door. She received no reply so she tried the doorhandle. Finding it unlocked, she raced through to the rear of the house where the bedrooms were.

'Arthur?' she called again, and this time received a reply.

'Mallory?' Arthur's voice was strained and worried as he stepped out into the hall. Without giving Nick a glance, he motioned to the bedroom. 'She's in here. It's bad,

Mallory. She's in so much pain.' He quickly crossed back to his wife's side and laid a tender hand on her brow.

'Has she vomited?' Mallory went around to the other side of the bed.

'Yes. Just after I called you.'

'How long ago did she take the painkillers?' It was Nick who spoke and Arthur gave Mallory a questioning look.

'You remember Nick Sterling. He's Appleton's new general surgeon. If Rose needs an operation Nick will be doing it.'

Her quick explanation seemed to satisfy Arthur who replied to Nick's question. 'About two hours before I called.'

Mallory stood back and allowed Nick access to Rose.

'I'm Nick Sterling,' he said softly. 'Can you tell me where it hurts the most?'

'Everywhere. Up here.' She raised a shaking hand to her right side. Nick prodded as gently as he could but the pain it caused was too great.

'Pethidine,' he said over his shoulder to Mallory, who quickly flipped open the black doctor's bag she'd brought in from the car and began drawing up a shot of the analgesic drug.

Once the pethidine began taking effect, Rose relaxed and closed her eyes.

'I'd like to get her to hospital for an ultrasound to begin with,' he said to Arthur.

'What's that?'

'Ultrasound scanning provides us with a painless way of examining internal organs. It sends a stream of very high-pitched sound through the tissues of the body. These sounds are then deflected off the internal organs and converted into a picture that we can see on a screen,' Mallory explained, as she rounded the bed and placed a hand on Arthur's shoulder in comfort.

'So you don't need to cut her?'

'Not for the ultrasound.' Nick shook his head slightly. 'It will at least give us an indication of what's happening to Rose's gallstones then I'll know what treatment is required.'

'Have you packed a bag for her?' Mallory asked.

'Yes.' Arthur pointed to an old leather case that sat in the corner of the room.

'Right. I'll get the ambulance and her admission organised.' She gave Nick a nod and left the room.

Placing her bag on to the kitchen table, Mallory sat down and withdrew her mobile phone. Punching the programmed number for the ambulance, she waited to be connected. Nick walked in and stood at the table while she made the call.

When she'd finished, Mallory looked up at him. 'That's the ambulance done—now for the hospital. I'll organise a bed and ultrasound scanning.'

'Good. How long will the ambulance take?'

'Around ten minutes maximum.' She looked at Nick and grinned. 'So much for starting work on Monday, eh?'

'What are a few days here and there? At least I've already been appointed as a consultant to this hospital so I don't need to worry about any paperwork, before operating.' He looked down at Mallory and returned her smile. 'And to think I'd hoped for a bit more peace and quiet in moving to the country.'

'Welcome to the real world, Mr Sterling,' Mallory quipped with a teasing smile.

Arriving at Appleton General Hospital, Mallory pulled up behind the ambulance and handed her keys to Garth, one of the orderlies, who would park her car in the doctors' car park. Nick had ridden in the ambulance with Rose and Arthur, and once Rose had been transferred on to a hospital barouche they wheeled her directly to Radiology.

'Do I have to go in?' Arthur asked, his face rather ashen.

'Not if you don't want to.' Mallory eyed him carefully. 'Are you feeling all right?'

'It's hospitals,' he admitted as he slumped down into the chair Mallory had guided him to. 'I have an…aversion to them.'

Mallory nodded in understanding. 'Just sit here and relax. We'll take care of Rose. Would you like a cup of tea?'

'I don't think I should have anything just now.'

'OK. I'll go and see what's happening with the ultrasound. Try to relax.'

She left Arthur with his eyes closed and a worried frown creasing his forehead. He was only a few years older than his wife but it seemed that, after the shock of his wife's illness, he was aging by the minute.

Nick was discussing the procedure with the radiographer as the ultrasound progressed. His expression wasn't one that foretold good news.

'Bad?' she asked softly, so as not to disturb Rose who was lying on the bed with an arm flung across her eyes.

Nick nodded. 'The pethidine is helping her through the pain for the moment, so I'd like her to be admitted to the ward while I get things organised.'

'I'll see to that.'

'Thanks. It's difficult being in a hospital where I don't even know people's names.'

'That's why they wear name badges.' Mallory grinned. After leaving the room, she spoke to the triage sister. As it was now almost ten o'clock the staff had thinned down, with the night shift settling in.

Once the admission had been organised, Rose settled in as comfortably as she possibly could, a concerned and sickly Arthur beside her.

Mallory led Nick to the doctors' lounge. 'How big are

the stones?' she asked as he held the ultrasound images up in front of the viewing box.

'One is a few millimetres but the other one—here...' he pointed to the screen '...measures almost one centimetre.'

'Lithotripsy?'

'I want to try it first before I operate. It may mean the difference between performing surgery or letting nature take its course.'

'You don't sound too positive,' Mallory said quietly, and watched as Nick rubbed his jaw with thumb and forefinger, studying the ultrasound.

'In nature taking its course? No, I'm not, but I'm also not the type of surgeon who's scalpel-happy. With controlled pain relief we have at least twenty-four hours to try and break the stones down, using lithotripsy, so they can pass out naturally through the bowel.'

'But...' Mallory prompted.

'But if they don't, I suggest we remove the gall bladder completely. Rose is in a high-risk category with her age and weight, and even if the lithotripsy is successful, the chances of this not happening again are very slim.

'So, if the lithotripsy doesn't work, it would be best for Rose if the entire gall bladder is excised?' Mallory questioned, making sure she understood.

'Precisely. I can remove it laparoscopically. That way, Rose only has a few small incisions with minimal sutures to contend with. Her recovery will be faster and less painful.'

'Why don't you head back to Radiology and get the lithotripsy treatment ready while I explain the procedure to our patients.'

'Patients?' he queried, emphasising the plural.

Mallory smiled. 'Poor Arthur has a problem with hospitals. He's quite unsettled.'

'Perhaps you should suggest he goes home and gets

some rest. If I need to operate, it won't be for another twelve hours at least.'

'I'll let him know.' Mallory smiled and walked out of the room. On the way to the ward she marvelled at her feelings toward Nick. She respected him one hundred per cent as a professional and was glad of the chance to be able to work with him.

Thoughts of the past and of Suzannah had no place in the hospital, where they were doctors with patients to be concerned about, and the neutral ground suited her perfectly. There was a spring in her step as she rounded the corner into the ward.

When she entered Rose's room she found Arthur sitting in the bedside chair, holding his wife's hand as though his life depended on it. Rose was soothing him, telling him everything would be fine. She gave Mallory a tired little smile.

'I keep telling him to go home. He's doing me absolutely no good, being here in this condition. It only makes me worry about him more.'

'I won't leave you, Rosie.' Arthur sat back in his chair, his face deathly pale.

'You may as well go home and get some rest, Arthur.'

'Is it good news, Mallory?' Rose asked, her eyes half-closed with drowsiness from the pethidine.

'Mr Sterling—Nick—wants to try a technique called lithotripsy. From the ultrasound we've discovered you have two very large stones which are causing you this pain. Lithotripsy is a method of breaking down the stones into smaller pieces, using an ultrasonic shock wave. There's no surgery involved in this treatment and if they're broken down small enough they may be able to pass out through your bowel quite naturally.'

Rose sat forward a little while Arthur seemed to slump further down into his chair with all this 'medical' talk. 'Is there a good chance that could happen?' she asked hopefully.

'To be honest, Nick isn't too confident, but surgery is our final option—not our first.'

'I'd like to try this lith— trippy thing,' Rose said decisively.

'Great. Nick is getting ready now, and once you've had a treatment we'll want you to rest. So you may as well go home, Arthur, and get a good night's sleep.'

'Mallory's right. I'll be fine as fine can be, snoring my head off. Think of all the peace and quiet you'll have at home.'

Arthur gave his wife a weak smile and said teasingly, 'It is tempting. I won't know what to do with myself.'

'Oh, get away with you.' Rose gave him a playful tap.

'Shall I ring a taxi for you, Arthur?' Mallory asked, and he nodded. 'Good. I'll send an orderly to wheel you back to Radiology Rose.'

'Thanks, Mallory,' they said in unison, and she left them alone to say their goodbyes.


'It hasn't worked,' Nick said the next morning to Mallory as he paced the floor in the doctors' lounge.

'Did you get any sleep last night?' Mallory asked. She knew he'd been home to shower and change. His hair was still slightly damp and his aftershave was whirling through her senses like an addictive drug—one she could get used to.

At that moment she was glad to be sitting down so that her legs didn't have to support her swooning body. Her eyes followed him eagerly, wishing she had the right to touch him and help take away some of his distress.

'Not much,' he replied.

'How was Rebekah this morning?'

Nick's grin was automatic at the mention of his daughter. 'Delightful—as usual. You should drop by later to see her.'

'I'll try.'

'It's Saturday, Mal. Don't tell me you've got patients to see?'

'Only two and a mound of paperwork. I'd also like to stay and see Rose through the operation, if that's all right with you.'

'Of course it is.' He scowled. 'You don't need to ask. As the referring doctor, I'm glad you have not only the time to spare but the desire to see your patient through. That's one thing I've always preferred about country doctors. They have more time for their patients.'

'Another reason why you moved back?' she asked softly.

'There are many reasons and, yes, that's one of them.'

'So tell me all that's happened with Rose.' When Mallory had arrived at the hospital and there had been no sign of Nick, she'd checked on Rose and had received a briefing from the ward staff. However she wanted to hear the official verdict from Nick.

'The lithotripsy was successful, as you know, in breaking the stones down into smaller pieces, but from the scan I did earlier this morning it doesn't look as though they're small enough. I could wait another twelve to twenty-four hours but it's not fair on Rose to have that pain, or to be on pethidine for pain relief.

'The gall bladder will have to be removed via laparoscopy. I'd like to discuss it with Rose and have the operation set in six hours maximum.' He stopped pacing and glanced at his watch. 'It's now ten o'clock so if I book Theatre for four o'clock this afternoon that should give plenty of time for fasting.'

'I don't think it's healthy for the surgeon to go without food for such a long period of time—especially when he has to operate,' Mallory teased, and received a wonderful, heart-stopping smile from Nick.

'The patient, Mal, not me.'

'Oh. Glad to hear it. For a moment there I thought I'd have to set Arlene onto you.'

He smiled and Mallory was pleased she'd been able to lighten his mood a little. 'Rose will be fine. She has the best general surgeon in Australia.'

Nick reached out and pulled Mallory to her feet. 'Thank you.' He bent his head for a kiss.

Mallory closed her eyes, her heart jumping into her throat as her reaction to the tenderness of his lips coursed through her body. One…two…three more little kisses before he put her from him. She gave him a frown, wondering why he hadn't deepened the embrace.

'Timing,' he answered her confusion. 'Timing is everything.' He glanced at his watch again. 'Come with me. It's time to explain the operation to Rose and see how Arthur is doing.'

He walked to the door and held it open. Mallory went through and together they went to the ward, each absorbed in their own thoughts.

'You've obviously reached a decision,' Rose said when they both entered her room. 'And from the look on your faces it's surgery.'

At Rose's words Arthur slumped further into the chair he occupied. Mallory crossed to his side and reached for his hand.

'Everything will be fine, Arthur. Rose will have a small operation this afternoon and then she'll be home within forty-eight hours. Nick and I need to explain the operation to Rose. If you'd prefer to go for a walk outside, so you don't feel nauseous, that's fine.'

'Mallory's right, Arthur. Get some fresh air while we talk things through.'

He gave a weak nod and allowed Mallory to help him. When she returned, Rose smiled. 'I feel so responsible for his condition. I know he can't stand hospitals, they've always made him queasy. At the sight of blood he usually faints dead away. Yet even when he sits beside me in that chair I feel so much better.'

'How long have you been married?' Nick asked, as he finished looking at Rose's chart and replaced it at the end of her bed.

'Forty-one years.' She smiled proudly.

'Then it's no wonder you need him to sit by you, and although he may not feel too good he's determined to be here.' He paused for a moment then glanced at Mallory. 'Let's get down to business and explain this operation. From what you've told me, the pain relief seems to be working well but you must notify the nursing staff if things change.'

'I will.' Rose folded her hands in her lap and waited for Nick to continue.

'I would like to tell you I can remove the stones easily but unfortunately I can't. You are in what we term a high-risk category. This means that even if the stones *had* passed naturally, thanks to the lithotripsy, the chance of new stones forming is increased.'

'What type of chance?' Rose asked, her eyes widening at Nick's words.

'About a ninety per cent chance. There is always that ten per cent that it would never happen again had the stones been small enough to pass through naturally after the lithotripsy treatment.'

'Well, believe me, Mr Sterling, I have no desire to keep having this type of pain,' Rose stated.

'OK. The only decision now is to completely remove the gall bladder.'

'Can my body function without it?'

'Yes. As I'm sure Mallory has explained to you at your earlier check-ups, the gall bladder is a pear-shaped sac located next to the liver. It's used for the storage of highly concentrated bile, which is secreted by the liver. The bile is then injected into the duodenum which connects the stomach to the first part of the small intestine.

'After removal of the gall bladder, you will no longer be able to produce gallstones or store bile again. However, the bile continues to reach the intestine by means of the hepatic and common bile ducts which are also attached to the liver.'

'Basically,' Mallory said, 'the bile just takes another pathway.'

'Sounds good to me.' Rose nodded. 'If my body can function fine without the gall bladder, let's get rid of it.'

'Good.' Nick smiled at Rose's blunt manner. He crossed to her bedside and gently folded back the covers. 'I'll be making two small incisions, what we term ''portals'', about a centimetre long in the abdominal wall. I'll make one here.' He pointed to the left side of Rose's abdomen. 'And one just above your naval. These allow me to pass instruments across to reach the gall bladder and remove it, using a laser scalpel. Very neat and very clean.'

Rose waited for a few minutes and then looked at Nick. 'That's it? Two little cuts?'

'Yes.'

She frowned at him. 'Why do I get the feeling there's more coming?'

Mallory smiled. 'Apart from fasting immediately, the only other thing we do is to inflate your abdomen with gas once you're sedated. That will allow Nick to manoeuvre the instruments with more ease. However, there is a side effect to the gas.'

'You'll get an aching pain in your shoulders which can be relieved with hot packs. The nursing staff will make sure you have a good supply,' Nick finished.

Rose waited for a moment and looked from one doctor to the other. 'Is that all? Pain in the shoulders? I've had bigger pains than that before.' She chuckled to herself. 'After giving birth naturally and raising twin boys for the past thirty years—who were relatively big pains in the neck—I think I can stand a bit of shoulder pain.'

'What a woman.' Nick laughed. 'I only have one relatively small pain in the neck,' he said jokingly, and Mallory protested.

'I'd hardly call a two-and-a-half-year-old angel a pain in the neck.'

'Oh, I wasn't talking about Rebekah,' he teased, and pointed a finger at her. Rose laughed at the two of them, then clutched her side as the ache increased.

'Don't make me laugh,' she warned. 'Pethidine or no pethidine, it still hurts at times.'

'Right.' Nick replaced Rose's bed covers. 'Let's get things organised, Dr Newman.'

'So you'll be there, Mallory?' Rose asked with a hopeful expression.

'Of course I will be.'

'Good. Then I'll probably see you both in Theatre this afternoon.'

'The anaesthetist will be around in another hour or so to see you. In the meantime,' Nick said as he walked to the door and held it open for Mallory, 'we'll see if we can track your husband down.'

'Better take a wheelchair with you,' Rose suggested, and they agreed.

Mallory waited while Nick informed the nursing staff of the operation. Walking casually to the theatre block, she noticed he was in a better mood.

'The nursing staff will send an orderly to find Arthur and return him safely to Rose,' Nick told her.

'I'm sure Rose will appreciate that—even if Arthur

doesn't.' She paused for a moment before saying, 'You're decidedly happier than before.'

'I was concerned Rose might have been upset that the lithotripsy wasn't successful. Thankfully, I've discovered her to be an intelligent woman who understands the prescribed treatment, making my job that much easier to perform. Now I need to speak with the anaesthetist and prepare the theatre.' He stopped in the corridor and looked at her. 'Didn't you say you had a few patients to check on?'

'Yes.'

'Why don't you do that now and meet me back here half an hour before surgery? That way, all your paperwork and jobs are done.'

'Makes sense,' she agreed.

'Then you'll be free afterwards and can't turn down the plans I've made.'

'I see. I suppose these plans include Rebekah and therefore, as you well know, I couldn't possibly refuse.'

'See? Neither of us has changed that much, Mal.' He leaned in closer and looked deeply into her eyes. 'We can still read each other's thoughts.' With that, he planted a quick kiss on her lips, then turned on his heel and continued towards the theatres.

Mallory tried as hard as she could to put Nick Sterling out of her mind as she made her two house calls. The first one was to check on Chloe Hone, who had just had her third child. Mallory sat at her kitchen table, sipping a cup of tea while Chloe fed little Nathan.

'He feeds and sleeps well—just like my other two.'

Mallory smiled at the woman opposite her. 'That's wonderful to hear.'

'After everything I went through with Joshua, having the emergency Caesarean, the other two have been a breeze.'

Nathan finished feeding and Chloe handed him over to Mallory so she could bring up his wind.

The tiny newborn was almost weightless in her arms and Mallory nuzzled him in closer to her shoulder and gently rubbed his back. 'Babies always smell so yummy,' she said.

Chloe laughed. 'He does at that end but the other end…' They both laughed and Nathan's mother sat back and drank her tea.

'You look healthy and relaxed,' Mallory said softly.

'I feel it,' Chloe replied. 'Damian is a wonderful father and a very supportive husband. I don't know where I'd be without him. He's just taken Josh and Louise to pick up some lunch and a video which should keep them entertained for a few hours. They'll be back soon—would you like to stay for lunch?'

Mallory was rewarded with a loud burp from her charge and smiled as she felt his little body relax even more. 'Is he asleep?' she whispered.

'Yes.'

'Good. Thanks for the offer but I have to see Jessie McFarland, catch up on some paperwork and then I'm due at the hospital around three-thirty. If I don't keep going, I'll never get everything done.'

'I don't know how you do it.' Chloe shook her head then stood to collect her son.

'Thank you for the cuddle, Nathan.' Mallory gave him a soft kiss, before handing him back to his mother. 'Thanks for the tea and I'll see you next week. Put him in his cot— I can see myself out.'

'See you next week,' Chloe confirmed and walked off to the bedrooms.

Mallory stopped at the shops and picked up a sandwich for lunch, along with a piece of delicious macadamia fudge. Today she would have to forego her delicious ice-cream treat but the fudge would fill the void and, besides, the sugar fix would get her through the afternoon.

Jessie McFarland's home was on the outskirts of town, an old house that had been there for as long as Mallory could remember. She pulled up in the driveway and climbed out of her car with her black doctor's bag in one hand.

Jessie met her at the door and held out an arthritic hand in welcome. 'I wasn't expecting you so early but it's a delightful surprise. Can you stay for lunch?'

Mallory took the elderly lady's hand in hers but shook her head at the same time. 'I'd love to but I have quite a bit to get through this afternoon. I've just been down to your granddaughter's sandwich shop and will eat my lunch when I'm catching up on my paperwork.'

'At least if you're eating one of Brittany's sandwiches, I know you're eating right. I worry about you, gel.'

'Thank you.' Mallory was touched by the other woman's concern. 'Here.' Mallory reached for the screen door and held it open. 'Let's go inside and get your check-up out of the way so we have more time to chat.'

'Good idea.' Jessie reached for her walking stick and shuffled slowly inside. 'I've been feeling so much better, and when I went to Brisbane to see Dr Barclay, the rheumatologist, he was very happy.'

'That's wonderful.' Mallory had received the same news in her report from Dr Barclay a few days previously, but she wasn't going to spoil Jessie's good news by saying so. 'Your gait is so much better since that last hip replacement,' Mallory commented as she watched Jessie walk past her. 'When are you due to see the orthopaedic surgeon?'

'Not for another three weeks.'

'Good. Let's get on with this check-up.' Mallory pulled out the sphygmomanometer to check Jessie's blood pressure. Ten minutes later they were sitting at Jessie's old kitchen table, sipping iced tea.

'I hear that Nicholas Sterling is back in town,' Jessie said matter-of-factly, as though trying to gauge Mallory's reaction.

'Yes, he is. He's taken up the position of general surgeon.'

Jessie gave Mallory a narrow glance. 'I hear he's brought his little girl with him.'

'Yes.' Mallory began to feel uncomfortable under Jessie's penetrating gaze.

'I know she appeared to be your friend, dear, but Suzannah Martel was a spoilt child from the day she was born. Whatever she wanted, her elderly parents gave her.' As Mallory squirmed in her chair Jessie reached out a hand. 'I don't want to bring you any unnecessary pain, dear, but I've lived in this town all my life and, believe me, in eighty-five years you see a lot of people come and go.

'I always had time for your mother and was sorry to see her go back to England to live when your father died. At the time you began dating Nicholas she was very worried about you, not because she thought he was wrong for you— quite the contrary—but she had noticed Suzannah's jealousy. Then when everything turned around and Nicholas married Suzannah, your mother was beside herself with worry over you. It must have been an extremely difficult and heartbreaking time for you—and now he's back.'

'Yes. He's back,' Mallory acknowledged in a choked whisper as she tried to regain emotional control of herself. 'I had no idea Mum was worried.'

'She was and as she's not here to look after you now that Nicholas has returned, I'm appointing myself your guardian. If that man hurts you again, he'll have to answer to me.'

Her words brought a smile to Mallory's lips. 'He's not *that* bad.'

'You've obviously seen him,' Jessie prompted.

'Yes.' Mallory shook her head in wonderment. 'Everything seems to be happening at a rate of knots. He invited me around to dinner last night and introduced me to his daughter.'

Jessie's eyebrows shot upwards. 'He certainly doesn't waste any time.'

'His housekeeper, Arlene, was there,' Mallory added, as though trying to justify having had dinner with a widower in his house with only his two-and-a-half-year-old daughter as chaperone.

'I have no doubt she was. What's his little girl like?'

The smile on Mallory's lips, reached her eyes as she thought of Rebekah. 'Adorable. She has beautiful brown curls, about the same colour as my hair, and blue eyes like her father's.'

'Sounds as though you've fallen in love.'

'I have,' Mallory answered absently, then looked at her companion. 'With Rebekah,' she clarified quickly.

'Of course.' Jessie nodded, then held out her arthritic hand to Mallory. 'Just be careful and know that I'm here for you whenever you need me.'

Mallory took her hand. 'Thank you, Jessie. That means a lot to me.'

'Now, you'd better be on your way, gel. You must be starving and that paperwork must be done.'

'Yes, it must.' Mallory collected her bag and, as Jessie insisted on walking her to the door, waited patiently for her to do so. 'You're a wonderful friend.' Mallory gave Jessie's cheek a kiss.

'I look on you as one of my own—my fourteenth granddaughter—and I always take care of my own.'

As Mallory drove away from Jessie's home, she reflected

on what had been revealed about Suzannah. Had Mallory
been completely blind to her friend's real motives? Surely
not. They'd been friends for so long and Suzannah had
always seemed so genuine. She'd always told Mallory that
no one had understood her like she had and that had been
why their friendship had meant so much to her.

But if her mother had had reservations as to Suzannah's
character, then perhaps Mallory *had* been deceived. The
other revelation from Jessie had been that her mother had
approved of her dating Nicholas Sterling...

With her thoughts and emotions completely jumbled,
Mallory felt exhausted. She parked the car in her reserved
space at the clinic and went into her surgery to finish the
outstanding paperwork.

After eating her sandwich and nibbling on her fudge, she
began to feel slightly better. The paperwork, though tedi-
ous, had done the trick of soothing her ruffled feathers. She
glanced at the clock on the wall and realised if she didn't
hurry, she'd be late for Rose's surgery.

It was definitely Rose she was concerned for, she told
herself as she drove to the hospital. At least be honest with
yourself, she chided. Her heart wasn't racing for her patient.
Her fingers weren't impatiently drumming on the steering-
wheel because she was anxious that Rose's surgery would
start without her.

It was Nicholas Sterling who was causing her pulse to
accelerate. It was Nicholas Sterling who had her in such a
dither that she couldn't wait to see him again. To touch
him again. To kiss him again.

Pulling into the car park, she quickly clambered out of
her car and locked the door. She almost ran to the front
door but forced herself to walk briskly instead. She knew
Nick would be in the doctors' lounge and without a glance
at anyone else she raced straight for that room. Bursting
through the door, she stood stock-still as Nick looked up

from the text he was reading. A smile spread across his face and Mallory felt herself slip completely under his spell.

Although she might have a million unanswered questions regarding the past, there was one question that had just been answered without a doubt. She was as much in love with Nick Sterling as she had ever been—in fact, probably more so.

# CHAPTER FOUR

'IS EVERYTHING all right, Mal?' Nick asked when she didn't move from the door.

Mallory looked at him for another heart-stopping second, before realising she needed to pull herself together—and fast!

'Uh…sure. I mean, no. Nothing's wrong. Why? Why should something be wrong? No, everything is just fine. Just fine.' She spoke quickly—too quickly. She crossed to a chair opposite him and closed her eyes for a moment, taking a deep breath. When she opened her eyes Nick's frown had deepened.

'You're acting strange, Mal. Who were the patients you had to see?'

'Chloe Hone and Jessie—'

'McFarland,' he finished for her. 'I see. She was never one of my biggest fans. What did she say about me?'

Pleased he'd assumed that was the cause of her weird behaviour, Mallory managed to slow the frantic beating of her heart back to normal and answered his question teasingly,

'You certainly have a high opinion of yourself, Nicholas, if you think you're the topic of every conversation in this town.'

'But I am,' he stated. 'Tell me I'm wrong, then. Tell me old Mrs McFarland didn't have something to say about me.'

When Mallory didn't reply he nodded. 'See. I'm right. I'm always right. You'd do well to remember that.'

'Yes, Nicholas,' she answered demurely, her eyes dancing with merriment. A few minutes in his company and she felt as though she were on top of the world. Such was his hold over her.

'Stop teasing,' he demanded, and looked her straight in the eye. 'Spill it, Newman.'

'OK.' Mallory smiled. 'She simply said that if you hurt me again you'd have her to answer to.'

'Appointed herself your guardian, has she? Well, her concerns are unfounded. I have no intention of hurting you, Mallory.' He stood and came around to stand in front of her. Slowly he pulled her to her feet, placing his hands on her shoulders. 'In fact, if the truth be told, I plan to make you happier than you've ever been in your life.'

Mallory swallowed hard at his words, her brown eyes as wide as saucers. What exactly did he mean?

'Got it all figured out, have you?' she asked in a whisper, trying once more to regain some control over her emotions.

He must have read the apprehension in her eyes because he gathered her close to him, cradling her head against his chest.

'Mallory,' he said. 'Just relax.'

The door opened and a theatre sister walked in. Mallory tried to push Nick's arms away but he would have none of it. He slowly released her from his hold, before turning to see who had disturbed them.

'Rose is ready for you to see in Theatre Two.'

'Thank you,' Nick replied, before taking Mallory's hand in his and tugging her out of the room. 'Time to scrub,' he told her.

She tried to pull her hand out of his but only succeeded in causing Nick to tighten his hold. If she didn't want to make a scene, looking like a schoolgirl being dragged reluctantly along, then she'd have to go along with it.

She increased her stride so they were side by side. Nick turned and smiled at her. She could feel other staff members watching them, the gossip starting the instant they'd passed by.

When they finally reached the scrub room Mallory wrenched her hand free, although she knew it was more the case that Nick had decided to release it.

'What do you think you're doing?' she muttered through gritted teeth. 'The gossip in a town this size is terrible. You should remember that.'

'I'm counting on it.' He nodded and switched on the taps to begin scrubbing his hands and arms.

Mallory digested this information. 'You...don't mind...' She couldn't finish the sentence.

'That people think we're an item? No. I don't mind at all. In fact I prefer it.'

Mallory's temper began to rise at his audacity. 'And what if I were involved with someone else?'

'He'd soon be out of the picture. People are probably dredging up old memories from the last time I lived here. I just thought I'd give them something else to add to their gossip.'

'Which is...?' Mallory waited, eager to see what he said.

'The fact that you and I are together—again.'

'I see.' She clenched her jaw, before saying, 'Did it ever occur to you to ask *me* if I wanted to be...connected with you? After all, you were married to my best friend. Perhaps I don't choose to have Suzannah's leftovers.' Her temper was in full spate.

'Mallory,' Nick said sternly, 'firstly, I do not like being referred to as ''Suzannah's leftovers'' and, secondly, she's been dead for two years now. I know this might sound heartless and no doubt fit in with the ''villain'' image you have of me, but I've been given a second chance at happiness. I'm not about to let it pass me by—again. So let me give you some advice—this time around, try trusting me.'

He elbowed the taps off and watched as Mallory finished scrubbing her own arms. When she looked up at him his eyes showed anxiety and she immediately felt sorry for her attack.

The scrub nurse came to help them gown so any further conversation was suspended. Upon entering Theatre, both of them pushed personal feelings aside, allowing their professionalism to take over.

'Hello, Rose,' Nick said with a smile in his voice. 'We meet again.'

Rose gave him a weak smile, groggy from the premedication. She was transferred from the barouche to the operating table.

'Everything will be fine,' Mallory assured her. 'See you when you wake up.'

Rose closed her eyes as the anaesthetist administered the injection that allowed Rose to slip into unconsciousness. The area where the incisions were to be made was prepared and draped.

Once the anaesthetist had given Nick a nod, the gas was inserted to inflate the abdominal wall.

'Would you mind turning the monitor a little bit to the left?' Nick asked the scout nurse, who was the person who could touch anything nonsterile. 'Ready to incise,' he announced, and as Mallory was only there as a spectator she watched everything Nicholas did from the right of him.

The endoscope was passed through the first portal. Mallory still marvelled over modern medicine and technology. The endoscope was a steerable, flexible, cylindrical instrument with fibreoptics for illumination and viewing. The one Nick was using contained channels to allow washing and suction of the area being examined.

The laser was passed through the second incision site and Mallory watched the monitor as Nick guided it to the gall bladder.

'Mallory, come here and hold this for me,' Nick ordered, and Mallory was instantly by his side.

'Here…' He handed her the endoscopic light. 'I need to insert the clamp.' Through the first portal Nick passed another endoscopic instrument, but this one had a small clamp attached to the end. 'Hold it firmly in place. It takes great expertise to set these instruments in exactly the correct place,' he murmured as he concentrated, then added, 'I hope you're suitably impressed.'

'Without a doubt,' she replied, her gaze fixed on the monitor.

Once all the instruments were in place, Nick was able to place the clamp around the top of the gall bladder, before dissecting it away from the liver. After gradually removing everything and checking the bleeding points, Nick made a small stitch in each of the portals to close them up.

'Thank you, everyone,' Nick announced to his theatre staff before he started de-gowning.

Mallory followed him out of Theatre and once they were alone she asked, 'Why did you get me to assist? You had a perfectly competent assistant there who ended up being the spectator.'

Nick shrugged. 'I didn't want you to miss out on the fun.'

'Nick,' Mallory implored.

'Look, I'm sure Dr whoever he is won't mind. Besides, how often is it that you get to go into Theatre? I thought it might make it more interesting for you if you could participate, as well as watching. Didn't it?'

'Well…yes,' she admitted reluctantly. 'But that's beside the point.'

'Don't want to consider a career as a surgeon? I could get used to having you by my side in Theatre.'

'Thanks but, no, thanks. I'm quite happy with my job, but that still doesn't change what happened.' Mallory had to concentrate hard on her words. That reference to being by Nick's side had caused her heart to pound fiercely. *Any* time she was close to him the same thing happened.

'I will apologise to Dr whoever if it will make you any happier. Besides, by the end of this year Dr whoever will be so sick of doing laparoscopies that he'll be glad of one less experience.'

'Yes. Do apologise to Dr *Wylie*. After all, it's the right thing to do.'

'Do you always do the right thing?' he asked softly, taking one of her hands in his. He gently played with her fingers for a second, while waiting for her answer.

Slowly Mallory withdrew her hand. 'I kept away from you for the past five years.' Her voice was soft and she lowered her gaze.

'And you think that was the right thing? I beg to differ.' Nick placed a hand under her chin and raised her head so their eyes met. 'Everything is going to change, Mal. For the better. Trust me.'

The look in his eyes was a promise. She wasn't exactly sure what Mr Nicholas Sterling had planned for her, but if she remembered anything about Nick it was his attention to detail. Whatever it was, he had obviously thought it out so thoroughly that, as far as he was concerned, nothing would go wrong.

Unable to hold his gaze for much longer, fearing she would crumble and throw herself into his arms, Mallory took a step backwards, breaking the contact.

'I…' She swallowed, her mouth and throat suddenly dry. 'I…um…have to…uh…get going.'

'Where?' he asked, an indulgent smile on his lips. It was as though he knew how badly he affected her, that he could read her mind.

'Somewhere! Anywhere!' She took another step away from him, as though forcing herself to put physical distance between them would help her keep her emotional distance. Her newly discovered love for Nick was more powerful than it had been when she'd been twenty-five and Mallory desperately needed some time to come to terms with it. Being in his presence, it made her forget her sanity—along with everything else.

'All right. You may have half an hour to go home, shower and change.'

'For what?' A frown creased her forehead.

'For our date. Remember?'

She tilted her head to one side. 'Did you actually *ask* me or did you just *tell* me?'

'I told you Rebekah would be there, which means you can't afford to say no.'

'You play dirty, Nicholas.'

His smile was triumphant. 'Ain't it the truth? It's now almost...' he consulted the clock on the wall '...five o'clock. Be at my house within half an hour, Mallory, or I'll come looking for you.'

'I don't think I'll even dignify that statement with a response,' she replied haughtily, before turning on her heel and walking away from him.

Mallory didn't know why she allowed him to rile her. Nicholas knew of old how to stir her temper and then extinguish it with one of his mesmerising smiles.

The problem was, he knew he was right. Anything to do with Rebekah was of the utmost importance to her. He'd invited her to spend all the time she wanted, getting to know his daughter, and Mallory intended to do just that.

She walked out of the hospital into the early dusk. The sun would soon set but the weather was still very pleasant for this time of year.

Officially the end of winter, the Sunshine Coast, which was where Appleton was located, was generally a few degrees cooler than the popular Queensland beaches. A

twenty-minute drive down through the tree-lined hills that
Mallory loved so much took them into the heart of the
tourist area where people all over the country came to relax
and enjoy the famous beaches that lined the entire state's
coast.

Climbing into her little car, Mallory drove home to her
empty house. A feeling of loneliness swept over her, and
for the first time in ages she regretted not having a house
filled with the colour and laughter that children gave and a
husband waiting eagerly for her return.

There was vibrancy in the hallways of Nick's house.
Rebekah filled them with giggles, squeals and delighted
laughter. When Nick arrived home tonight he would be met
with cuddles and kisses from the little girl who adored him.

Mallory slowly undressed and switched on the shower
taps. Stepping under the spray, she finally allowed the dam
to burst and the tears rolled down her cheeks, being washed
away by the water.

She cried as she had all those years ago when she'd
learned of Nick's betrayal. It had been Suzannah who'd
broken the news to her. Suzannah had come over, tear-
stained mascara on her face, and had told Mallory about
the 'mistake' that had happened.

Mallory had just arrived home from Brisbane for the
weekend. Those precious days away from the hospital
where she had just started her internship had meant everything to her. Nick, too, had been working at the hospital
but had been home a few days before Mallory arrived.

Suzannah had met him at the local club where they'd
had dinner together. They'd talked and laughed like the old
friends they'd been, not keeping count of how many drinks
they'd had.

'Nick told me it was bliss not being on call for Theatre
and therefore able to drink as much as he wanted,'
Suzannah related. 'I guess we really drank a lot because…'

She hung her head, a little sob escaping her lips. 'Well, I…um…' She stopped again and took a deep breath. 'We slept together.'

At Mallory's shocked expression, Suzannah continued quickly, 'I can't say that I remember a great deal as I was so drunk, but in the morning I woke up—naked—in his arms.'

Mallory remained silent and Suzannah went on. 'I quickly dressed and left. I'm so embarrassed and…I'm so sorry.'

Mallory's distress and disbelief at what she was hearing disturbed her beyond comprehension. Nick? *Her* Nick? With *Suzannah*? Her *best friend*?

'It was a mistake, Mallory,' Suzannah clarified quickly. 'A huge mistake. But I thought…well, I thought you had a right to know.'

An uncomfortable silence surrounded the two friends as Mallory forced herself to continue to breathe in and out. Suzannah broke the silence.

'That's not all.'

Mallory clenched her teeth and waited.

'I, well, I checked the calendar and, well, it's not a safe time to have had unprotected sex.'

If Mallory had thought she was stunned before, it was nothing compared to now. Suzannah might be *pregnant*? With *Nick's* child? The room began to revolve slowly and Mallory hoped that at any moment she would wake from this horrifying nightmare. Betrayed by the man she loved most in the world *and* her best friend.

Mallory finally broke her silence and whispered, 'I can't believe it. I can't believe it. Not Nick. This just isn't *like* him. He hardly ever drinks as much as you've said he did.'

Anger, hurt, rejection, bitterness—they all ripped through her body in a rage.

'And *you*! Suzannah, how could you? You're my best

friend. We've been friends...for ever. How could you betray me like this?'

Suzannah had burst into tears at Mallory's words. 'I didn't have to tell you. Nick and I could have kept it a secret but I know how you hate deception. Besides, I feel guilty enough. It was a mistake, Mallory. We were both drunk and...' The sobs grew louder and Mallory felt her anger toward Suzannah ebb out of her body. She sat down beside her friend and placed an arm about her shoulders.

Slowly, Mallory's head began to clear. It had happened—now they had to deal with reality.

'Suzannah, you'll need to see a doctor. We'll go to the clinic together and you can see my father. He'll know what to do.'

'No!' Suzannah had been adamant. She flatly refused to see a doctor. 'I don't want anyone else to know, Mal. It's too...humiliating.' After a bit more persuasion from Suzannah, Mallory agreed to keep silent. Suzannah, however, agreed to performing a home pregnancy test herself, in a few weeks when the results would show.

'I'll buy it at the shopping centre near the beach—that way the whole town won't know.'

'Good idea,' Mallory agreed.

Some weeks later, Mallory's world stopped revolving on its axis. The pregnancy test, Suzannah informed her, was positive. After finding out they'd made love Mallory had refused point blank to see or speak to Nick.

He'd begged and pleaded that she tell him what was wrong. Mallory, unable to face him, wrote him a long and detailed letter after the pregnancy was confirmed.

She even read it to Suzannah over the phone to make sure it sounded final. Knowing that her friend was carrying Nick's child, it meant that she *had to* give Nick up. She urged him to marry Suzannah as soon as possible so his irresponsible behaviour and its consequences could be hushed up as much as possible.

Suzannah came down to Brisbane to see Nick, and not long after that they married. Mallory begged her father to pull all the strings he could to transfer her internship from Brisbane to Sydney. There was no way she could have worked in the same hospital as Nick. The gossip alone would have killed her, let alone running into him.

On the night of the wedding, after suffering through the humiliation of being Suzannah's bridesmaid, Mallory was involved in a terrible car accident...

Washing her face and giving her body a more than vigorous scrub, Mallory turned off the water. She felt drained, rehashing the old memories, the old hurts. The anger, the bitterness and the dejection had sucked all the life from her—much as it had done all those years ago.

As she towelled herself dry, Mallory was still unable to believe that her love for Nick had only grown with time. Even though he'd hurt her so cruelly, she knew deep down in her heart that she forgave him.

Suzannah... Well, Suzannah was another matter. Mallory still missed hearing from her friend but realised that during the years before her death, all Suzannah had done had been to complain. She'd always been a pessimist where as Mallory had always been an optimist.

After hearing Jessie McFarland speak so disparagingly about Suzannah and indeed, relate Mallory's mother's misgivings about the girl, Mallory wasn't sure *how* she should think of Suzannah any more.

Nick, however, seemed to be just the same. Mallory was under the impression that throughout the course of his marriage Nick had grown distrustful and resentful, but as she took the hair-dryer out and started drying her hair Mallory knew he was just the same.

*Her* Nick.

She wasn't sure whether she wanted to see him right now, with the old memories so fresh in her mind, but she knew he *would* come looking for her if she didn't show up at his house by five-thirty.

Resolving to put her thoughts back onto a more even keel, Mallory finished drying her hair and dressed in a long, bright, floral dress, making sure she took her jacket with her. After all, it was still technically winter.

She knew Rebekah would like her bright dress and this was her main motivation for wearing it. It wasn't because it showed off her figure or that she knew Nick would appreciate it as well, although for a very different reason.

Nick had suggested a truce concerning Rebekah, that they put their past and present differences aside and just enjoy the company of the little girl they both loved so much.

And that was exactly what Mallory intended to do.

# CHAPTER FIVE

MALLORY rang the doorbell and waited. No answer. She knew Nick was home because his Jag was in the driveway. She rang the bell again. Still no answer. She had arrived at twenty-five past five—five minutes early—but surely Nick wasn't going to keep her waiting until *exactly* half past to let her in?

Tentatively, Mallory placed her hand on the doorknob and turned it. She was surprised when it moved and she gently pushed the door open.

'Hello?' she called loudly into the stillness of the front rooms. No answer.

Mallory closed the door and walked down the hallway towards the kitchen. 'Hello,' she called again, and this time she heard Arlene's voice answer her. She followed the sound.

'Sorry,' Arlene said as she came through the back sliding door, holding a huge basket of washing. 'I was outside the back and didn't hear the doorbell. I'm glad you came through. I left it unlocked specifically for you.' Arlene took the basket through into the laundry and left it there.

When she came back out she said, 'From now on, why don't you just come around here to the back of the house?'

'OK,' Mallory replied, secretly pleased with the privilege.

'Nick's upstairs with Rebekah. Why don't you go on up and say hello?' Arlene suggested.

'OK,' Mallory repeated, and with a smile at the other woman she turned and went up the stairs. When she got to

the top she heard a high-pitched squeal, followed by lots
of giggles.

The sound warmed Mallory right through and an invol-
untary smile lit her face.

The door to the room from where the sounds were em-
anating was slightly ajar. Mallory knocked and slowly
pushed the door open. Stepping into the room, she realised
with a start that this was a very masculine room—Nick's
room.

The giggles increased, along with calls of, 'Stop it,
Daddy. Stop it.'

'Is there a tickle in your…tummy?' Nick asked, before
the sounds of a raspberry being blown on Rebekah's stomach filled the room, along with more squeals of laughter
from the toddler.

Rebekah was lying on her father's bed, squirming
around, while Nick's lips seemed to be stuck to her stomach. Nick was wearing faded denim jeans—and nothing
else. Mallory's heart pounded and her mouth went dry as
she looked at him.

The jeans fitted him perfectly, moulding themselves to
his shape. She slowly exhaled, feeling her palms begin to
sweat. His back was bronzed and his hair was being tousled
by his daughter's little fingers.

'Stop it, Daddy,' she squealed again, and he lifted his
head. Mallory knew she should say something but her mind
refused to work. Instead, she just stood there, watching the
way he moved, the way he laughed, the way he so loved
his little girl.

'You're a monkey,' he told Rebekah.

'No. You a monkey, Daddy,' she said cheekily. She
squirmed again and managed to break free from his loose
hold. Rebekah stood and looked over her father's bent head.
'Hey-yo,' she said with a smile on her face when her eyes
met Mallory's.

Nick immediately turned around, straightening as he did so. 'Hi, Mal.' He greeted her with a devastating smile and Mallory leaned back against the wall as she felt her knees begin to weaken.

'I'm almost ready,' he said as he reached out a hand to tickle his daughter again. 'I just got a little bit distracted.'

Mallory couldn't say a word. She was positive her brain had completely shut down. She simply couldn't take her eyes off Nick. He sported a washboard-like stomach, a firm chest and his arms… Mallory swallowed convulsively and closed her eyes momentarily, unable to meet his gaze. Her eyes snapped open again when she felt his lips brush softly over her own, lodging her breath in her throat.

'Hi,' he said again, this time as a whisper. She saw a burning desire in his eyes and knew instinctively that it mirrored her own.

'Kiss me, Dad.' Rebekah had climbed off the bed and come to stand beside them, tugging at Nick's jeans. 'Kiss Becka,' she demanded.

Nick's smile spread across his face, the desire extinguished immediately as he bent to scoop up his daughter.

'Hey-yo,' Rebekah said again when she was brought up to Mallory's eye level. 'Kiss Becka, Daddy,' she ordered, and was obeyed as her father planted kisses all over her face.

'You're a scallywag, Rebekah Mallory Sterling,' he announced as he moved to dump her on the now messy bed. He blew another raspberry on her squirming stomach, her laughter once again filling the room.

The momentary reprieve allowed Mallory to engage her brain and pull herself together.

When Nick had finished, Rebekah pointed to Mallory.

'Your turn now,' she instructed, and patted the bed. 'Lie down.'

'What?' Mallory's eyes turned to Nick's for an interpretation—and she hoped it was different from the one she'd come up with.

Nick smiled and looked at his daughter. 'Is it Mallory's turn to have Daddy tickle her tummy and blow raspberries?'

'Yes,' Rebekah replied, then she looked at Mallory again and said. 'Lie down, Malwee. Your turn.'

'Thank you, darling,' Mallory said with a big smile on her face, although she was dazed at the thought of Nicholas tickling and blowing raspberries on her stomach. She was already on fire deep within from that fleeting brush of his lips over hers. If he actually lifted her dress and blew a raspberry on her stomach…

Mallory almost hyperventilated at the thought. Nick was dangerous enough by himself, without any assistance or suggestions from his daughter.

'But Daddy needs to get dressed.'

'Spoil sport,' he chided, his eyes twinkling with merriment. 'Mallory's right, blossom. We're going for a ride in the car so you'd better get your blue sandals and ask Mallory to put them on for you. Then you need to go to the toilet and then we need to get the basket of food from Arlene.'

'Yay! Go in the car,' Rebekah shouted with glee, and raced passed Mallory into her bedroom to find her sandals.

Mallory and Nick were left alone in the now silent room.

'I'm very good at blowing raspberries, Mal,' he told her, his tone seductive but teasing. 'You have no idea what you're missing out on.' He advanced slowly towards her and as she was already leaning against the wall she had no where to run.

'I think I'd like to keep it that way,' she retorted, trying not to respond to the magnetism he exuded.

Nick placed a hand on either side of her head, barricading her in. The teasing smile was still on his lips as he slowly lowered his head and kissed her briefly again.

'Glad to see you're on time, Dr Newman,' he whispered, before he kissed her again, this time with more pressure, more pleasure, more passion.

Mallory opened her mouth to his, giving in to the moment. A gentle sigh escaped her as she wound her arms around his neck, taking *her* turn to run her fingers through his already tousled hair.

Nick shifted his weight, sliding one hand slowly from the side of her breast down her waist to the top of her thigh and then back up again. His thumb gently rubbed under her breast and Mallory shivered with longing.

She untangled her arms and took her turn at sliding her hands over the smooth contours of his warm skin—down the front where she walked her fingers around the waistband of his jeans to his back and then gently scratched her nails back up to his neck.

Nick groaned and broke the kiss. 'You remember how to torture me.'

'I could say the same about you,' Mallory responded.

Nick placed some small kisses on her face and then worked his way around to nibble briefly at her ear lobe, before blowing a soft raspberry against her neck. Mallory's skin broke out in goose-bumps and she shivered a little.

'Much as I'd like to continue, I'm afraid now is not the time, although this would definitely be the place.' He turned and looked longingly at his bed as he spoke.

Mallory cleared her throat. 'I…I'll, um…go and put Rebekah's shoes on.'

'Good idea.' Nick grinned at her as he watched her walk out of the room. She was getting closer, he thought as he pulled a polo shirt from the closet and put it on. A few times today he'd caught her looking at him with a dawning realisation on her face.

'Slowly and patiently,' he told himself as he combed his hair. As far as he was concerned, they'd already wasted too many years, but he knew that if he rushed Mallory she'd run from him for ever.

They still had unresolved issues to work through, Nick's main issue being why she hadn't trusted him all those years ago. But in time…in time the *real* reason for his move back to Appleton would be revealed to Mallory.

That reason being that Nick had chosen her as his future bride.


Nick had chosen a delightful spot for the picnic. It was a small park, tucked away near a popular beach. There was equipment for Rebekah to play on, leaving Mallory and Nick some time to talk alone.

'That was delicious,' she told Nick as she lounged back on the rug. 'Arlene is a gem.'

Nick agreed. 'She always seems to know just what to pack. Tonight was definitely a cold chicken and salad kind of night.' He picked up the bottle of wine. 'Would you like some more?'

'Just half a glass, please,' she consented. 'Rebekah certainly likes her food. It's not always easy to get a toddler to eat.'

'She has her days. A few months ago she would only eat breakfast so Arlene made sure it was a breakfast packed with as many of the five food groups as she could. Besides, as long as they drink enough fluids they won't waste away.'

Mallory sighed. 'She's so adorable, Nick. You're a lucky man.'

'Kids are incredible. Naturally they have good days and bad days, but her tantrums are few and far between.'

'Rebekah?' Mallory joked. 'Have a tantrum?'

Nick smiled. 'It's been known to happen but it's always when she's tired. As long as she gets enough sleep, she's usually a very happy girl. I feel that kids really help parents put their priorities in order. You should try it some time, Mal.'

'What? Putting my priorities in order?' She held his gaze, knowing exactly what he meant.

'I know you used to want children. Has that changed with the explosion of your hectic career?' There was a slight bitterness to his tone. Back when they had been dating, they'd often talked about having children one day.

Mallory swallowed, unable to get rid of the lump that had just formed in her throat. 'I like children, yes,' she agreed, 'but the time isn't right for me to start a family at this stage.' She shrugged nonchalantly.

'When would be the right time?' Nick asked, his tone a bit more urgent.

'I don't know. I just know that this isn't it.' Her voice had been more harsh than she'd intended. Tears sprang to her eyes and she turned her head, looking away from him out to the spectacular sunset. How in the world could she tell him about her disability? That, thanks to the car accident on the night of his wedding, the possibility of her conceiving a child naturally was basically zero. Crushed reproductive organs didn't do much for her chances.

Nick obviously took the hint. 'Majestic, isn't it?' He looked out at the beautiful colours in the sky. The oranges and reds blended together with a few white stratus clouds.

'Red sky at night, shepherd's delight,' Nick quoted.

'Red sky in the morning, shepherd's warning,' Mallory finished. Nick stood and held out a hand to her. Mallory eyed him for a moment, wondering at his motives before placing her hand in his. Nick pulled her up and gently reached out a hand to wipe away the tears that had settled on her eyelashes.

'I won't pry,' he told her softly. 'Soon, I hope you'll trust me enough to tell me.'

'Daddy,' Rebekah called. 'Come push Becka, Daddy. Come push Becka,' she chanted, jumping up and down next to the swing.

'Duty calls.' He shrugged, giving Mallory a lopsided grin.

Revelling in the delight of Rebekah being pushed on the swing, Mallory stood to the side of the play equipment and clapped and tickled the little girl as she swung to and fro. The complex world of the adult had often puzzled Mallory in the past. Why couldn't they all take things in their stride, just as kids did?

The seemingly carefree existence that children had should be captured for as long as possible. At least, this was what she had thought until Suzannah had shown up on her doorstep that horrible morning over five years ago.

Mallory had realised that when adults did stupid things the consequences could often be disastrous. Nick had broken her heart, shredded it into tiny little pieces. It had taken her a long time to come to terms with his defection and just when she'd thought everything had been right with her world he'd returned.

Thinking back over the past forty-eight hours, Mallory found it hard to believe how quickly Nick had woven his way back into her life. He didn't deny the past years of his marriage to Suzannah—Rebekah was evidence of that union—but he did seem to deny everything that Suzannah had ever done.

Was she herself somehow blinded by prejudice? Had Suzannah been lying to her for all those years? The complex nature of the situation confused her the more she tried to decipher it.

Why couldn't she just allow herself to enjoy Nick as she was enjoying Rebekah? Why didn't she simply let Rebekah's infectious and innocent attitude envelop her? She *loved* Nick, for crying out loud. She wanted desperately to be with him—to be with his daughter—permanently. Why couldn't she let herself acknowledge openly her true feelings?

Because he might hurt you again, a small voice from within whispered. She might love him but trusting him again was a whole new ball game.

'Mal?' Nick spoke softly beside her.

Mallory turned her head sharply and looked at Nick.

'Are you all right? You were miles away.'

'Sorry.' She looked down at the swing, amazed to find it empty. Her eyes quickly scanned the playground. Rebekah was climbing up the ladder to the slide.

When she reached the top she called to them, 'Watch Becka.' Then she slid down and landed in a heap at the bottom, giggling as she did so. She stood up and clapped. 'Clever Becka.'

'Yes, clever Becka.' Nick clapped as he walked over to pick up his daughter. 'Now, darling, it's time to go home.'

'No,' Rebekah said emphatically, and started to squirm in his arms. 'No, Daddy. Becka wants to stay and play.'

'It's getting late,' Mallory chimed in as she came to stand by father and daughter.

'Say goodbye to the playground,' Nick instructed. 'We'll see you soon.'

Reluctantly, Rebekah waved her little hand to the inanimate objects. 'Bye-bye, paygound. See soon.'

'Let's go home and find Arlene.'

'Yay, 'Lene.' Rebekah clapped. 'Find 'Lene, Daddy.'

'We need to pack up first,' Mallory reminded them. 'Will you help me, please, Rebekah?'

'Yes. Help Malwee. Pack up.' She squirmed in her father's arms again and this time Nick let her go. She ran over to the rug where all three of them had eaten and began tugging at the end of the fabric.

Mallory hastened her step and rescued the already

packed picnic basket from the rug before Rebekah could
upturn it. Nick helped Rebekah to fold the rug and then
allowed her to 'help' him carry it back to the car.

'Me help Daddy,' she told Mallory as Nick stowed everything away in the boot.

'You're a very clever girl,' Mallory told the toddler,
bending down so she was at Rebekah's eye level. 'You're
a good helper, Rebekah.'

'Tank-oo,' Rebekah said, and leaned forward to give
Mallory a hug.

The action was completely voluntary and Mallory's arms
automatically wrapped themselves around the small, warm
body. Her heart warmed, her lips quivered and her eyes
filled with tears again—but this time they were tears of
delight. Rebekah had accepted her.

The embrace lasted only a moment before the child
pulled away and allowed her father to strap her safely into
her car seat. 'Click-clack—front and back,' she chanted as
he did so.

Mallory straightened and wiped her eyes. She wondered
if her wayward emotions would ever settle down when she
was around Rebekah. The child represented everything
Mallory would miss out on in not becoming a mother.

'Amazing, isn't she?' Nick asked as he shut Rebekah's
door. 'I know how you feel. It still gets me right here.' He
pointed to his heart. 'Every time she hugs or kisses me.
There are some things that we just shouldn't take for
granted.'

'Mmm.' Mallory nodded, her emotions too extreme to
manage speech. Nick reached for her hand and squeezed it
momentarily, before opening her door and waiting for her
to climb inside.

The drive home was made in silence—at least by the
adults. Rebekah, on the other hand, listened to her favourite
nursery-rhyme tape and sang along with all the songs.

When Nick pulled into the driveway, Rebekah was impatient to be out and finding ''Lene'. Nick let her scamper out of the Jag and she raced into the house, calling for the woman who was as close to a grandmother as she'd ever have.

'Thanks,' Mallory said when he held the car door for her. 'I had a lovely time, Nick.'

'You're not going to come inside for coffee?'

She smiled and shook her head. 'The last time I did that I received an emergency call. I don't think I want to chance it again.'

He returned her smile. 'You have to say goodnight to Rebekah. She'll be worried if you don't.'

'OK,' Mallory agreed, and followed him into the house.

After staying a few minutes to chat with Arlene and receiving another hug and kiss from Rebekah, Mallory allowed Nick to walk her to her car.

'Thanks. I had a lovely time.' She was starting to feel a little nervous at being alone with him. Nick had a way of making her feel as though everything would turn out right—but that was the way he'd made her feel all those years ago and back then things hadn't worked out the way she'd planned.

'You've already said that,' he pointed out as he stood in front of her.

She opened the door to her car and put her bag inside. 'Rebekah is wonderful.'

'You've said that before as well.'

'Well if everything has been said, I should be going.' Mallory turned her back on him and inserted her key into the ignition.

'Mallory.' He placed his hand on her arm and urged her gently around to face him. 'Why are you so nervous?'

'I'm not nervous,' she replied quickly. 'Who said I was

nervous? I'm not nervous.' Why was she trying to refute it? She even sounded nervous to her own ears.

'You forget, Mal, that I know you too well. Tell me what the problem is.' Nick took her hands in his.

'You said you wouldn't pry,' she responded immediately, and Nick shook his head.

'I'm not talking about *that* problem, Mal. I'm talking about why you're so nervous around me. It's just me. Good ol' Nick.' The smile he gave her was electrifying and Mallory felt its full force throughout her body all the way to the tips of her toes.

Mallory returned his smile and then sighed. 'I don't know, Nick. I guess things are moving just a little too fast for my liking. I mean, I only bumped into you yesterday morning and in the past forty-eight hours I seem to have spent most of my time with you.'

'Not all of it, believe me,' he growled with a smile. 'There were some vital hours that we *could* have spent together that we definitely didn't,' he teased.

'Nick, be serious.' She tried to but couldn't resist the smile he was trying to provoke.

'Look, Mal. I want to see you again. I want to date you. I want you to get to know my daughter. I don't care who knows about it but you're the person who needs to be comfortable with it.' He gave her hands a squeeze. 'I'll try and slow down, although you know how hard that will be for me.'

She laughed. 'Yes. You always did do everything at top speed.'

'Some things never change.' The words were spoken in jest but somehow they settled over them in a more serious manner. 'Some things never change,' he whispered again, before gathering her closer to him.

With agonising slowness Nick bent his head to claim her lips. It was as though he was trying to slow down already and he particularly took his time in the exploration of her mouth.

With tantalising expertise Nicholas gently nipped at Mallory's lips. Her eyelids fluttered closed, her knees grew weak and she sagged against his hold with relief. The tip of his tongue urged her lips to part a little more before the pressure of his own lips increased—ever so slightly.

Mallory sucked in a breath of air, filling her starving lungs before returning the softness of his caress with her own. She ran her tongue tenderly over his lips and then carefully eased her mouth away.

Her breathing became more ragged as the suppressed passion was re-ignited. She tipped her head back as Nick began to press faint kisses along her neck, dipping downwards towards her breasts. Although her dress was quite respectable, it revealed a hint of cleavage, but it was more than enough for Nick to torment her with until a groan of pleasure escaped from her parted lips.

Pushing one hand up to caress her scalp, Nick urged her head up so their lips could once again meet, the familiarity they possessed with each other evident in their actions.

Nick's patience seemed to have run its course as the pressure from his mouth turned hot and hungry. Mallory couldn't have been more pleased as she matched his pace with burning excitement.

She felt on fire but it was a feeling she was more than happy to experience. Nick had one arm about her shoulders, the other still laced through her hair, as he pressed her against the car, the length of his body hard against hers.

Mallory wound her arms tighter about his neck, wanting never to let him go again. This was the man she loved with all her heart, and she told him so with her kiss. She refused to allow her mind to dwell on the past. This moment—the feelings they were experiencing—was all that mattered.

Nothing else existed except the two of them. So right for each other.

'Mallory,' Nick whispered when he finally raised his head, his breathing as ragged as her own. 'Mallory. See how perfectly you fit into my arms.' He placed a few more kisses on her face as she clung to him. 'We were made for each other.'

They stood together for another few minutes, Mallory resting her head against Nick's chest, listening as the rhythm of his heart echoed the pounding of her own. She knew he was right. They were made for each other. Soul mates.

But there was still so much to work through and she would be duping herself if she allowed this frightening natural attraction to rule her actions.

When she could finally trust her legs to support her and her brain to function, Mallory gently eased herself from Nick and looked up into his hypnotic blue eyes.

'I need to go,' she whispered.

He nodded as though he understood, and she believed that he did. Kissing her briefly once more, he broke his hold and smiled.

'So much for slowing down.' He laughed.

'Mmm,' Mallory agreed, and returned his smile. 'We may need to work on that a little.'

'Does this mean you'll agree to be seen with me in public?'

'I hardly think I can avoid it after your display at the hospital this afternoon,' she retorted and he had the grace to look sheepish.

'Sorry. I couldn't help myself.'

'Try harder next time,' she suggested. 'I have to go.'

'Can I...? I mean we—that is, Rebekah and I. Can we see you tomorrow?'

'Sure,' she replied as she climbed into her car and shut

the door. Rolling down the window, Mallory started the engine. 'Church starts at nine-thirty. You can sit next to me—if you promise to behave.'

Nick smiled and crossed his heart before giving the Scout salute.

'Wrong hand,' she pointed out, and laughed as he quickly changed hands. 'Yeah, right. I know you weren't a Scout, Nick.'

Mallory put the car into reverse and Nick bent his head to meet hers at the open window.

'See you, then,' he said softly, his breath fanning her face as his lips met hers for one last time before he pulled away.

Mallory laughed, feeling like a schoolgirl all over again. 'Nicholas Sterling in church. This I've got to see.'

# CHAPTER SIX

OVER the next few weeks Mallory's life seemed to settle into an easy pattern.

One week after Mrs Koos had come to see her she bumped into her in Brittany's shop. Mallory had just scooped the first taste of her vanilla jelly-bean fudge ice cream into her mouth, her eyes closed as she once more savoured the flavours, when she heard Mrs Koos whisper to Brittany, 'It's a ritual. I think the whole town has seen her do this at one time or another.'

Mallory opened her eyes and smiled at the two women. 'It has a calming, soothing effect,' she defended herself.

'Nicholas Sterling must be doing *something* right,' Brittany told Mrs Koos. 'She's already been in twice today.'

Mallory simply continued to smile at them both, not giving away any particulars on her much-gossiped-about relationship with Nick.

'And how are *you* feeling, Mrs Koos?' Mallory asked quietly as Brittany moved away to serve another customer who had just come in. 'You haven't called or come back to see me so I'm presuming everything is fine.'

'Oh, yes, dear. I can't believe how wonderful I feel. Those herbal remedies are working wonders.'

'I'm so glad,' Mallory responded.

'I especially love that raspberry leaf tea. Delicious. I have several cups a day.'

'And the other problems?'

'Stopped. I think you were right when you said I was working myself up into a tizz over nothing.' Mrs Koos shook her head in amazement. 'You've saved my sanity, Dr Newman.'

'You make sure you come and see me if you have any queries or questions.'

'I will, dear. I must go. I have so much to get through.' Mrs Koos said goodbye and Mallory treated herself to another spoonful of her ice cream.

The following day she stopped by to see Rose who had been home from hospital for a few days.

'Everything is settling down nicely,' Rose told Mallory. 'Dr Sterling is happy with my progress but he's probably already told you that, what with you two being together.'

'Yes, he has mentioned it,' Mallory confirmed, but once more refused to pass on any extra gossip. 'How's the pain in your shoulders?' she asked.

'Completely gone. All settled. I have trouble standing up as my stomach muscles haven't quite recovered yet, but everything else is in working order.'

'Good. Now, how's Arthur?'

'Mollycoddling me to death. He's so thankful I'm home from hospital he's running around, making sure I have everything I need, just in case I overdo it and have to be readmitted.'

Mallory laughed. 'Sounds like Arthur. I'd better go. I promised Rebekah I'd stop by and take her to the park.'

'Becoming quite attached to that little girl, aren't you?'

'I'm lost, Rose. Hook, line and sinker.'

'And what about her father?'

'Oh, I expect he was lost the instant she was born. She has him wrapped around her little finger.'

'That wasn't what I meant, Mallory Newman, but I'll let it go this time.'

'Thank you, Rose,' Mallory replied with a smile. 'Take it easy.'

'Arthur wouldn't have it any other way.'

Most of her free time at weekends was spent with Rebekah, and if Nick happened to be there it was a bonus. Every second night Mallory would go around there for dinner and spend more time with Rebekah. Even if Nick was late home or, as had happened on one occasion, been caught up in Theatre and had missed her completely, Mallory still went.

Her relationship with Nick was still moving very slowly—at her insistence. He was allowed to kiss her but that was all. They would talk about a variety of topics and the few times that Nick had tried to talk about the past Mallory had simply said, 'Not yet, please.'

He was having trouble holding onto his patience, she knew, but she also refused to be rushed. Once he asked her straight out why she hadn't bothered to hear his side of the story. Why she had unquestioningly believed Suzannah. Why she hadn't trusted him.

Thankfully, on that occasion they were interrupted by an emergency, with Nick being called away to the hospital. Mallory returned home and thought about what he had said.

Why *hadn't* she trusted him? She thought long and hard about that question but only ended up giving herself a headache and another sleepless night.

On the more positive side she and Arlene had become good friends and between them enjoyed the company of the little girl both loved so dearly.

'Rebekah starts playgroup next week,' Arlene told Mallory one Friday evening as she put the finish touches to the dinner. 'It's important for her to have contact with kids her own age.'

'The one at the neighbourhood centre?' Mallory asked, and Arlene nodded. 'It's a good one. Lou-Anne McFarland—one of Jessie's granddaughters—runs the playgroup and she's well qualified.'

'I've checked it out thoroughly,' Arlene admitted. 'But

hearing you say that, it puts my mind even more at rest. I trust your judgement.'

This was high praise, coming from the usually reserved woman, and Mallory glowed with pride.

'Rebekah,' Arlene called, but the child didn't answer.

'I'll go and get her,' Mallory volunteered willingly, and went to the playroom where she knew Rebekah had been watching television.

Standing in the doorway, Mallory watched the small girl, who had dressed herself up in an old pair of ladies' shoes, a satin skirt, handbag, hat and a strand of pearls, as she danced around the room, singing the song currently being sung on the video.

She was incredible. The imagination process was in full swing and Mallory felt honoured to have witnessed such a charming sight.

'Mallory?' A deep masculine voice spoke just behind her, and she nearly jumped out of her skin. She spun around to see Nick loosening his tie and placing his briefcase on the floor beside him. Holding one finger over her lips, Mallory motioned for him to come and watch.

The two of them stood there for a few minutes, watching Rebekah dance around the room, singing out of tune, oblivious of her audience. When the song was finished Mallory and Nick both clapped and cheered.

Totally unabashed, Rebekah smiled up at them both, before taking a bow. 'Tank-oo,' she said. 'Tank-oo berry much.' Then, as though her feet had grown wings, she all but flew at her father, clamping her little arms around his legs and chanting, 'Daddy's home. My Daddy's home. Look, Malwee, my Daddy's home.'

Nicholas picked his daughter up with a groan. 'You're getting big, scallywag.'

'Either that or Daddy's getting older,' Mallory responded.

'Actually, my back is a bit sore today,' he said seriously, but there was a twinkle of mischief in his eyes as he gave Rebekah a tickle. 'Rebekah had a bad dream last night, so once she calmed down she slept in Daddy's bed until morning. Didn't you?'

Rebekah nodded, a cheeky smile on her face.

'She took all the covers and slept with her feet in my back so you could say that I received a good "kick start" to the day.' He tickled his daughter again, before hugging her close. 'Where's Daddy's kiss?' he demanded, and was rewarded with a sloppy kiss from Rebekah.

'Where's my kiss from my other favourite girl?' He turned to face Mallory as he spoke, the toddler still in his arms.

'Kiss for Malwee,' Rebekah screeched at the top of her lungs, and giggled when Nick once again tickled her.

'What a good idea.' He nodded his consent and leaned forward to give Mallory a brief but satisfying kiss on the lips. 'I could quite easily get used to this,' he said softly.

'Used to what, exactly?' she asked, knowing what he meant but wanting to hear the words all the same.

'Coming home to my family. You, Rebekah, Arlene. My girls.'

'Well I'm flattered, Nicholas,' Arlene said as she walked towards them, 'that you'd refer to me as one of your… "girls". I'm well over fifty, young man.'

'But that new anti-wrinkle cream you've been using does wonders for you,' he teased, and Arlene shook a finger at him.

'If you weren't holding Rebekah, Nicholas Fitzwilliam Sterling, I'd give you a hiding.'

'I bet you say that to all the boys,' Nick said with a laugh, and Mallory, still becoming accustomed to the teasing relationship Nick shared with his housekeeper, just smiled.

'Fitzwilliam?' she teased him softly a moment later when Arlene had taken Rebekah off to wash her hands before dinner.

Nick almost looked uncomfortable. 'Family name.' He shrugged.

She eyed him sceptically. 'You always told me you didn't have a middle name.'

'I lied.' He shrugged again and looked almost pleased when the mobile phone clipped to his belt rang. As if her own phone had ears, Mallory's mobile, nestled safely in her handbag in the kitchen, began to ring as well.

Walking back to the kitchen, she groaned, realising that if both of them were being called there must be an emergency somewhere.

Nick came into the kitchen, his phone clipped back on his belt, just as Mallory was ending her call.

'Do we have time to eat?' he asked, pulling the oven door open and breathing in the delicious smell of Arlene's shepherd's pie. 'I, for one, am starving.'

'Have you been called out?' Arlene asked as she and Rebekah came into the kitchen.

'Look, Daddy. Hands all clean.' She held her hands out for inspection, which Nick duly conducted before pronouncing them squeaky clean.

'We both have,' Mallory answered for him. 'A bad car accident about twenty minutes from here, heading inland.'

The housekeeper shook her head. 'Those roads are so winding.'

'Precisely.' Mallory shrugged.

'Well, you're both eating,' Arlene pronounced, and proceeded to rummage around for some containers. 'There's no way you can go into Theatre or do whatever it is that you have to do on an empty stomach. At least this way,' she said as she took the shepherd's pie out of the oven and served it into the containers, 'I know you've both eaten a healthy, well-balanced meal. None of that…hospital food for you two.'

'Yes, Arlene,' Nick replied with mock meekness. He picked his daughter up and gave her a cuddle. 'You're so nice and squishy, my Rebekah. Daddy loves you.'

'Wove oo, Daddy,' she replied, and gave him a kiss.

'Daddy and Mallory have to go to work now. You stay with Arlene and have some dinner. Then bathtime and bed time.'

'And teef-time, too,' she said.

'Oh, yes. Teeth-time in there as well.' He gave her another squeeze, as though he could never get enough of his little girl. 'Daddy loves you so much, Rebekah.' Another few kisses and he put her down. 'Give Mallory a kiss and cuddle goodbye.'

Mallory bent down to the child's height and felt the now familiar wave of longing and happiness envelop her as Rebekah's arms came tightly around her neck.

'Bye, Malwee.' A sloppy, wet kiss was planted firmly on Mallory's cheek before Rebekah let her go. 'See later.'

'Goodnight, darling. Sleep well and, yes, I'll see you later.'

Arlene had finished packing their 'take-away' and put the containers into a thermal bag to keep them warm.

'Make sure you've both eaten within the next half-hour or there'll be trouble,' she warned as she handed the bag to Nick.

'Mallory will eat first,' Nick told his housekeeper. 'The instant she gets to the hospital her job as head of the retrieval team will begin. I, on the other hand, can't do anything until I have patients before me. We'll take my car,' he added to Mallory, and walked out of the room.

Mallory said goodbye to Arlene and, after collecting her handbag, followed Nick out to the car.

Once she was seated and strapped in, Nick dug out one

of the meal containers and handed it to Mallory. 'Here,' he said, after giving her a fork as well. 'Eat on the way. You may get indigestion but it will be better than attending the crash site with a grumbling stomach.' He closed her door and came around to the driver's side.

'Your concern is touching, Nick,' Mallory said with a smile as she began to eat. 'Mmm, delicious.'

'Stop it.' His stomach growled in protest and Mallory laughed. 'The aroma of the food is hard enough for me to bear, without you adding comments.'

The hospital wasn't far from Nick's place and by the time he pulled into the emergency park bay Mallory was almost finished.

'Talk about shovelling it in,' she joked when she'd swallowed the last mouthful.

'At least I'll get a bit more time to savour my meal,' he retorted.

'On the contrary.' Mallory shook her head. 'As head of the retrieval team, I want you at the crash site with us.'

'But I'd be more use here,' he argued as they got out of the car. Walking in through the front door, Nick tossed his car keys to one of the orderlies who would go and park his car in the doctors' car park.

'Once Theatre is set up, Nick, there's nothing you can do until the patient arrives. That's a lot of wasted time when having you at the crash site would not only make my job a little easier but might also save a life.'

'What do you propose, Dr Newman?' he asked as they walked to Casualty where Stan and Jeremy—the other retrieval team members—were waiting for them.

'You'll find out. Just sit and eat,' she ordered, and collected the police accident report from the casualty sister.

'We're just waiting on Kate,' Stan told her as they made their way to the doctors' lounge. 'Knowing Kate, she'll be putting on her full make-up and doing her hair.' Stan shook his head. 'She's a brilliant nurse but there are some things about that woman I'll never understand.'

'Women are like that,' Nick replied, and the three men grinned.

'Shouldn't you be stuffing your face full of food, Mr Sterling?' Mallory asked sweetly, at which Nick sat down and dutifully began to eat.

'Right. I want the three of us to go in the first ambulance.' She indicated herself, Stan and Jeremy. 'Which should give Nick time to set things up here. Nick, you and Kate come in the second ambulance and by the time you get to the crash site I hope we'll have at least the first patient ready for you.'

'I'm sorry,' Kate said as she walked into the room. As Stan had stated, the blonde was immaculately made up and dressed. Too bad she'd be getting into the heavy duty, bright orange overalls they wore when out at an emergency. Even then, Mallory knew Kate would look exquisite.

'Kate, you'll be going in the second ambulance with Nick,' Mallory recapped.

Kate sauntered over to Nick, placed a hand on his shoulder and smiled sweetly. 'I *like* that arrangement.'

Mallory clenched her teeth as Nick looked up at the blonde and returned her smile.

'There are two people trapped in the car,' Mallory said firmly, indicating that she required everyone's full attention. 'Man and woman, early to middle twenties. The car, according to this report, is in a precarious position down the mountain slope. Exactly what that means we won't find out until we're there. We can assume the car has rolled so head injuries, seat belt injuries and mainly internal injuries is what we're up against. You all know your jobs and we're a fantastic team so let's put all our expertise and knowledge to the test and save those two lives. Let's suit up and move out.'

'Let's do it,' Jeremy said firmly, as he and Stan stood and left the room. Kate followed them out, leaving Mallory and Nick alone.

'Almost finished, Mr Sterling?' She came around to stand behind him as he finished off Arlene's meal. Placing her hand where Kate had previously put hers, Mallory began to massage his neck.

'You sounded like a coach a minute ago. What's the strategy?'

'Pumping everyone up. Adrenaline. We have no idea what we're going to find and, quite frankly, Nick, sometimes even the goriest scenes can still turn my stomach. Getting pumped up and preparing our minds mentally for what we'll find is important. It helps us to cope.'

Mallory stopped massaging and sat down in the chair next to him. 'How long is it since you've been out with a retrieval team?'

'Too long to remember,' Nick answered with a shake of his head.

'Well, then, Mr Sterling.' Mallory leaned in closer until she was only a few millimetres away from his face. 'You might even learn something.'

Mallory placed a kiss on his lips and then another one. She pulled back and looked at him. He was happily surprised at her directness.

'Are you dessert?' His tone was slightly husky, his eyes filled with desire. It was what Mallory had wanted to see—*needed* to see—after Kate's attitude toward him. Mallory wouldn't exactly have called it jealousy, but in the past few weeks she thought they'd made it clear to the whole town that they were dating again.

'I could be,' she replied, and kissed him again. 'But dessert will have to wait until later.'

Nick stood and pulled Mallory up against him. Wrapping his arms about her, he lowered his head and kissed her more thoroughly. It only lasted a few seconds but it cleared Mallory's doubts away.

'I'm not interested in Kate,' he whispered, and Mallory had the grace to blush. He knew exactly what she'd been thinking. 'Only you.' He kissed her fleetingly, before turning her from him to face the door. 'Now go and change.' She took a few steps away from him then he called her name. 'You *do* have a good retrieval team. You *are* a good leader. Those patients will come back alive, thanks to you and your team.'

Mallory smiled at him, her heart constricting with love. 'Thanks Nick.'

'Oh...my...goodness.' Mallory said each word slowly as she straightened from looking over the side of the mountain. 'Is the car stable?'

The policeman, who had been the first at the accident site, nodded. 'We've managed to get a cable around the front axle which will hold the front of the car quite firmly. Other cables have been attached to the driver's side, and the rear of the car is wedged firmly into the ground.' He held out his hand to her and she shook it briefly. 'I'm Senior Sergant Ryan and I'll be in charge up here.'

'Dr Mallory Newman. I'll be in charge of things down there.' She inclined her head to indicate the accident site.

The road had been closed off and the area was swarming with emergency personnel. Mallory looked again at the car which was lit by two huge floodlamps that the country fire service had set up.

The car had rolled a number of times and had finally come to rest on its side—passenger side down. As the policeman had informed her, the rear of the car had dug itself into the ground while the front was resting on an old gum tree.

As the country fire service personnel had managed to

secure cables around the car, if the tree branches gave way
the car would be suspended horizontally out from the side
of the mountain. At least so they had told her.

Mallory could feel her heart begin to pound in her ears.
She'd told Nick that it was the adrenaline that got them
through these situations and she realised that she was going
to need a heck of a lot to get through this one.

'What's the plan, Mal?' Stan asked.

They were all suited up with abseiling harnesses and
ropes, ready to scale down the mountain to the accident
site.

'The CFS have removed what was left of the front windscreen, which will make our job a little easier. They rec-
ommend getting the female passenger out first, and then the
driver. He's being held in by his seat belt and the steering-
wheel so once we remove those obstacles gravity will naturally pull him downwards. If the woman is out of the way,
we have more room to manoeuvre. These CFS guys know
what they're talking about and have already been down
several times so we heed their advice.'

Jeremy and Stan nodded.

'We need to have as little contact with the car as possible. They've said those cables will hold but I don't want
any unnecessary risks taken. If the danger is too great to
ourselves then we don't take the risks. Understood?'

'Yes.' Both men nodded.

'Stan, you go on the passenger side with the stretcher.
You'll need to get down lower than the car so when Jeremy
and I lower her out she can go straight down onto the
stretcher, rather than being winched upwards.

'Jeremy, you'll be with me, assisting with what I'll need.
The first order will be pain relief. There has been no sign
of consciousness yet, but when the CFS team checked both
patients were alive, their airways were clear and breathing
was not compromised.

'We stabilise the injuries as best we can and then secure the harness around her. Once she's ready we move her out. By the time she's up to the top Nick and Kate should be here. We'll have had a chance to assess the other patient but will probably need the foot pedals and steering wheel to be cut away before we can remove him.

'This is all speculation,' Mallory added. 'Let's get down there and see what reality has to offer.'

'Just a little lower, Mallory,' Stan instructed a few minutes later, as Mallory abseiled closer to the vehicle. The entire retrieval team were wearing headphone sets so that they could easily talk to each other, as well as communicate with the rest of the emergency crew up the top.

'To your right. Good. Now slowly.' Stan was already in position, below and off to the side of the car. From where he hung, secured by his ropes, he could see everything.

'Jeremy, stop for a second to allow Mallory to get into position. Mallory, a little more to your right.'

Mallory was just passing the rear of the car which was wedged into the ground. Unbelievable, she thought, but kept her focus firmly on her work. As the car was still balancing on some strong gum-tree branches, Mallory needed Stan's guidance to assist her through the maze.

'Watch that branch on your right. Good. Carefully find your way through.' Stan's voice was clear and calm. 'Good,' he encouraged her as she moved just below the smashed front windscreen. Securely held, Mallory was ready to work.

The driver was hanging by his seat belt, the steering-wheel effectively jamming him firmly in place. The woman was pressed against the passenger window, her own seat belt holding her securely. Thank goodness both had been wearing seat belts, Mallory thought, otherwise their services wouldn't have been required at all.

'Thanks, Stan. Talk Jeremy down while I take a look

around.' The light on her helmet illuminated the area but she reached into her top pocket for her small medical torch. Taking the woman's pulse, which was faint, Mallory quickly checked her pupils.

'Both the woman's pupils are constricting. Pulse is faint but present. There's a lot of blood,' Mallory reported. The woman was beginning to moan and Mallory instantly tried to calm her.

'You're going to be fine. Help is here. I'm Mallory—a doctor.' Mallory's voice was firm but gentle.

'I feel…weak.' Her voice was a whisper.

'What's your name?' Mallory asked as she waited for Jeremy to get into position.

'Uh….G-Gail,' the woman answered after a moment.

'And your friend? What's his name?' Mallory asked. It looked as though Gail was ready to pass out again, but before she did she said softly, 'Tom.'

'Jeremy, the instant you're ready I need the largest compression bandage you have. I'll also need a neck brace to keep her head stable. Our patient's names are Gail and Tom. Gail has severe lacerations to the abdomen. Extensive bleeding. I couldn't even *begin* to guess what's been ruptured. It looks as though something has gashed her right across her stomach. Query fractured pelvis.'

'I'm glad Nick's on his way,' Stan's voice said into Mallory's earpiece.

'I think we all are,' Mallory agreed. She felt Jeremy move alongside her. He let out a slow whistle as he took in the scene before him.

'Let's get to work,' he said, as Mallory edged around the broken windscreen. She was hanging right beside the windscreen, almost parallel with it, and was therefore able to reach around to treat Gail's injuries.

'What about Tom?' Jeremy asked.

'I can't get to him until we have Gail safely out of the

way. I don't want to risk scrambling over the bonnet to check him out. The centre of gravity of the car would change.' She shook her head. 'He's unconscious at the moment so, until the situation changes, we'll leave it at that.'

'Acknowledged,' Jeremy answered.

'I'll need to get that seat belt off her, before applying the pressure bandage.' Mallory leaned in through the open windscreen and very carefully, not touching the car, looked at the position of Gail's legs.

'Her legs aren't pinned at all. She's leaning quite heavily against the door so once she's harnessed we can release the seat belt. Then we'll bandage. Once that's done, we can move her immediately to the stretcher. Nick should be here by then and she can go straight up the mountain and into his care.'

'Good plan,' Stan concurred.

'Jeremy, hand me the harness and a neck brace before I get into position. Gail?' Mallory spoke clearly and firmly but received no answer. Checking the patient's pulse again, she discovered no change. 'Gail? I'm going to place a harness around you and then we'll start getting you out.' Mallory didn't know whether Gail could hear her but it was her custom to inform patients of the treatment and now was no exception.

Once the harness and neck brace were in place, Jeremy handed Mallory the heavy-duty scissors which would cut through the seat belt.

'Gauze,' Mallory ordered, as she returned the scissors and waited for Jeremy to place the large pad of thick gauze into her hand. She placed it over the woman's abdomen, applying pressure with her free hand, and taped it into position. 'I'll need at least three more,' she told Jeremy. Mallory repeated the procedure until she was sure everything would stay in place while they moved Gail to the stretcher.

'Ropes next,' she instructed. 'Ryan,' she said into the microphone fixed to her headset a few minutes later.

'Ryan here,' the police sergeant at the top of the mountain replied tersely.

'Gail's medical harness is attached to the ropes. Have your teams standing by. We're almost ready to move the patient to the stretcher below.'

'Will do.'

'Any sign of that second ambulance yet?'

'Just pulling up now.'

'Right,' Mallory acknowledged, and experienced a feeling of relief, knowing that Nick was there. Gail stood a better chance of recovery having a qualified general surgeon attend her injuries, otherwise, once they'd successfully hoisted the stretcher back to the top, Mallory would have needed to have spent time attending to Gail herself.

'Jeremy? Stan? Are you ready?'

'Yes,' both men replied.

'Jeremy, you'll need to come closer to help me support Gail. We need to keep her as horizontal as we possibly can. Ryan, get ready with the winch on the patient's ropes.'

'Standing by for your signal, Dr Newman,' the police sergeant reported.

'Gail,' she said softly, 'we're going to move you now.' The patient was still unconscious and Mallory hoped she stayed that way until she was safely at the top.

'On three.' She waited for a moment while Jeremy shifted his position slightly as per her instructions. 'One. Two.' She held her breath and offered up a silent prayer. 'Three!'

The winch started moving and slowly Gail was hoisted from the car and lowered, through careful and meticulous instructions from Mallory, onto the waiting stretcher. Once there Stan's job began as he ensured Gail's safety and double-checked her bandages.

'All clear, Mallory,' he reported. 'She's ready to move.'

'Right. Ryan, the stretcher is ready so start easing her up slowly. Stan, you accompany Gail up while Jeremy and I check Tom's situation.'

Soon Gail was halfway up the mountain with Stan rising steadily beside her.

'Jeremy. I'd like to take a closer look at Tom and check him out.'

'Be careful, Mallory.'

'I always am, mate.' She turned and smiled at the young RN. 'Thankfully the car didn't shift when we moved Gail, and as I'm roughly the same size I should be fine.'

Gingerly, Mallory pulled herself slightly up on her rope so her feet were hanging level with the car's open windscreen. Keeping her body as still as possible, she began to lower herself through the opening and into the spot Gail had recently vacated.

'I'm in.' She exhaled slowly with relief.

Stretching upwards, Mallory pressed two fingers to Tom's carotid pulse and found that it was slightly stronger than Gail's had been. Hopefully that meant he hadn't lost as much blood as she had.

She reported this. 'Pupils are constricting.' Mallory took a better look at how Tom was jammed in and sighed resignedly. 'The steering-wheel is all but sitting in his pelvis and his legs are well and truly jammed. Paraplegia would be my guess, and I sincerely hope I'm wrong.'

'Anything else you can do at the moment?' The voice that came through the headphones was Nick's, and Mallory felt a quiver of comfort wash over her.

'No. Is Gail at the top yet?'

'Almost. Both you and Jeremy come back up for a break. From what I've heard, the CFS people need a turn down there, cutting Tom free, before anything else can happen.'

'True. Give me a few minutes to manoeuvre out of the car and then we're ready to be winched up.'

'Understood.' Nick's tone was curt.

'Jeremy, I'm coming out now.' Mallory repeated in reverse the procedure that had allowed her into the car. She felt Jeremy's hand at her waist as she slowly lowered herself out of the car and back down beside him.

'Good work, Mallory,' he told her, and she could see the smile on his face. 'Now let's take a rest. My feet are itching to feel terra firma beneath them again.'

Mallory called Seargent Ryan and soon both she and Jeremy were being winched back up to the top.

'Whew!' she said as she stood and stretched. Removing her headset and releasing the harness from the ropes, she crossed to where Kate and Nick were absorbed in Gail's treatment.

'Basically, everything is ruptured,' Nick murmured when she knelt down beside him. 'I've stabilised her for the moment but it's going to require quite a bit of Theatre time to put her back together again.'

Kate had rigged up a saline drip and Nick had just finished packing the wounds and changing the dressing.

'When I took a closer look at her wounds,' Nick told Mallory as Gail's stretcher was transferred to the ambulance, 'I found small splinters of wood. I'd say that a roadside fence paling smashed through the windscreen as the car rolled and gashed Gail's abdomen.'

'Sounds consistent with the type of injuries she has.'

'It's a mess, Mal. Rig up a unit of blood, Kate,' he instructed the RN the instant Gail was in the ambulance. 'Do her obs for me again as well.'

'Yes, Doctor,' Kate replied.

'I'll let you go,' Mallory said just before Nick got back into the ambulance. 'I need to get back down to Tom.'

Nick's jaw tightened momentarily and he stared at

Mallory. 'I don't want you to go back down there. Surely the CFS guys can cut Tom out, wrap the medical harness around him and put him in the stretcher. Why do you need to go back down?'

'Nick,' Mallory warned.

'Look at you. You're exhausted. This is not only causing you physical stress but emotional stress. I know you're thinking—or trying not to think—about your own car accident.'

'Thanks, Nick.' Mallory said shortly, her anger at his behaviour increasing.

'See. I was right. You *are* trying not to think about it. You're in no condition to go back down that mountainside. From what you've said, there's not a lot you can do for Tom. All his injuries are internal. Let the CFS guys cut him out and hoist him back up.'

'This is my *job*, Nick,' Mallory said through clenched teeth. 'This is what I've been trained to do. Why don't you go and do what *you've* been trained to do and get out of my face?'

Mallory spun on her heel and started to walk away, but Nick's hand gripped her arm harshly.

'Mallory, I don't want you putting your life in danger— yet again. I couldn't believe the position of that car when I first saw it, and when I learned that you were actually *inside it* I nearly blew my top.'

'Let me go, Nick,' she said slowly, trying to hold onto her temper. 'The ambulance is ready to leave so I think you should go and attend to your patient.'

He held her gaze for a brief moment, the anger in his eyes reciprocating hers. Reluctantly, he let her go.

'You always were stubborn,' he remarked, before climbing into the ambulance. Mallory shut the doors firmly then turned and walked away.

# CHAPTER SEVEN

MALLORY replaced the headset and double-checked the rope attached to her harness.

'Ready to go?' Jeremy asked, and she nodded.

'Mountainside rescue, take two,' Stan said, as they all slowly walked backwards over the edge. Two CFS crew members, Frank and Richard, were still at the site and had almost managed to get Tom free.

'He's regained consciousness again,' Frank reported. 'You're all right, mate,' Mallory heard him tell Tom. 'You'll be out of here soon.'

Mallory followed her previous route down and, after navigating the branches of the gum tree, positioned herself alongside the windscreen.

'Tom?' she said softly.

'He's gone again, Doc,' Richard told her. Both he and Frank were on the other side of the car. They had carefully removed the driver's door, which had been winched back up to the top, and were steadily working on the foot pedals and steering column.

'You can put that medical harness on him now,' Frank instructed. 'I'm almost done, and once I am it will only be the seat belt that's holding him in.'

'That won't do his injuries a lot of good, being suspended by the belt,' Jeremy remarked as he came alongside Mallory. Stan was once again beneath them with the stretcher.

'The plan is to get the medical harness and neck brace on to him, release the seat belt and steering-wheel at the same time and then lower him out of the car the same way

we did with Gail.' Mallory knew she was going over old
ground but it helped to clarify things in her mind. They all
knew the plan. They all knew their part. Now all they had
to do was implement it.

'I need to get into the car,' she told Frank and Richard.
'Last time the car didn't shift so let's hope it remains stable.'

'We'll just move over a bit and out of the way while
you get in,' Frank replied.

When they were in position, Mallory once again hoisted
herself up by the rope and eased herself into the car.

'I'm in,' she reported, and took the small medical torch
from her pocket. 'Good. There's no change to his pupils.
They're still reacting to light stimuli. Pulse is slightly
weaker. Harness, Jeremy.' It was a bit more difficult to
secure the harness around Tom as Mallory had to stretch
up higher to do it. Gail had been at her level but Tom was
seated above her.

Finally, after slow persistence, she had him secure. Frank
and Richard moved back into their previous position and
resumed cutting the steering column away from Tom's legs.

'Jeremy. There's going to be a jolt on the ropes once
they take Tom's full weight. Gravity is against us. You
need to be as close as you possibly can to help get him
out. I think I should stay in the car to help manoeuvre him
through the windscreen.'

'Gail?' A dry, raspy voice asked.

'Gail is fine, Tom. I'm Mallory, a doctor from Appleton,
and we're trying to get you out of here as quickly as we
can.'

He seemed to relax at this news and slipped back into
unconsciousness again. Mallory checked his pulse. Getting
weaker still.

'We need to move faster. His pulse is weakening rapidly.
How much longer, Frank?'

'A few more minutes will do the trick.'

'Ryan,' Mallory called into the headset. 'Do you copy that?'

'Few more minutes,' Sergant Ryan's voice repeated. 'We're ready for your signal, Doctor.'

The minutes seemed to tick by with agonising slowness. Once time was up, though, Mallory knew everything would happen at once.

'Scissors, Jeremy,' she instructed, and waited for him to pass them through to her.

'I'm done,' Frank reported. 'We'll hoist it up and out through the windscreen. That's when you cut the belt.'

'Understood,' Mallory acknowledged, and cut the belt the instant the steering column was out of the way.

Tom's body weight shifted into the harness with a jolt— and so did the car.

Mallory let out a choked yell, her heart hammering in her chest with fear, as she heard the branches beneath the passenger side of the car snap under the weight. As her rope was clipped securely in place she couldn't move, her head colliding with the already bent roof of the car.

Then everything stopped. Everything was still again and Mallory realised the cables were holding the car, as well as herself and Tom. She breathed a sigh of relief, her head still pounding from its sudden contact with the roof.

'Everyone OK?' she asked as she slowly lowered herself down a fraction. There was a chorus of affirmative replies.

'How about you, Mal?' Jeremy asked.

'Just hit my head, but other than that I'm fine. Let's get Tom out of here while we still can.'

Jeremy came alongside and carefully guided Tom out and onto the waiting stretcher. Once Stan and Tom were safely clear of the tree branches, Mallory ordered everyone else back up.

'With pleasure,' Frank retorted. 'I'm sure that shift gave us all a fright. Especially you, Doc.'

'Especially me,' Mallory concurred. 'I'm glad it's over. Now for the next part of the rescue. Keeping Tom stable until we reach the hospital.'

By the time they reached the hospital Tom was still managing to hold his own. The ambulance doors were opened by the orderlies and the stretcher wheeled into Casualty.

'Dr Newman?' a tall, blond man asked, but didn't wait for Mallory's nod. 'I'm Dr Thornton Gray, a colleague of Nick's, and this is Dr Susie Monahan. I'm a general surgeon, Susie's an orthopod,' he informed her as Tom was wheeled to an examination cubicle.

The relief on Mallory's face must have shown because Susie said with a smile, 'From what Nick's told us of the accident site, I'd say you've obviously been through enough for one night. We can take it from here.'

'Fine.' Mallory gave them an update on Tom's condition and suspected injuries. 'There has been no response at all from his legs to the standard tests. As you can see, we've cut his trousers off and dressed the lacerations and contusions to control bleeding but his pulse has been getting steadily weaker. He's had one unit of blood but, still, there's something not quite right.' As she spoke, both Thornton and Susie were examining the patient. One of the orderlies wheeled the portable X-ray machine into the room and the radiographer began preparing film.

'The steering-wheel was basically sitting in his lap so I can only hazard a guess at what you'll find.' As Mallory finished off her report and watched the experts at work, she realised that her work really was now done.

Tom's pulse rate had weakened but thankfully, after a blood transfusion, it stabilised. Mallory had been praying that Nick would be finished with Gail but knew, considering the extent of Gail's injuries, that it would be unlikely.

Thank God he'd had the presence of mind to call for reinforcements. Thornton and Susie had obviously been flown up to Appleton while they'd been busy rescuing Gail from the car.

'Come on, Mallory.' Stan placed an arm about her shoulders. 'Let's go and have a relaxing cup of tea.'

'Good idea,' Jeremy said.

The three of them left Casualty and walked towards the hospital cafeteria. Mallory slumped into a chair and allowed her body to finally relax.

'I think I ache all over,' she complained, and raised a hand to her head.

Stan crossed to her side and forced her to look at him. He checked her pupils, then had a look at her head. 'No bleeding, pupils are fine, but you're going to have a lovely headache from your collision with the roof.'

'Tell me about it,' Mallory whispered as the pounding inside her head began to increase. Now that she was relaxing the pain and stress her body had been through during the past few hours was beginning to make itself known.

'Take some paracetamol when you get home and soak in a hot bath,' Stan ordered as Jeremy placed a cup of tea in front of her. 'Drink it.'

Mallory did as she was told. There would be a debriefing later, after they'd all had some sleep and the sun was up again.

'Mallory? Mallory?' Jeremy called. 'Earth to Mallory.'

'Sorry.' She smiled sleepily. 'I think I should head home.' A yawn escaped, as though to verify her decision.

'I was just going to suggest that. Would you like a lift?'

'Lift? Oh, yeah,' she said with dawning realisation. 'I'd completely forgotten that I didn't have my car. Yes, thanks. That would be great.'

'You wouldn't prefer to wait around for Nick?' Stan asked.

'Who knows how long he'll be? No, thanks.'

'Right. Then let's get going.' Jeremy cleared away the cups and the three of them walked out to the young nurse's car.

'Uncle Stan, I think you'd better drive. My eyelids are almost closing as it is.' Jeremy handed over the keys as Mallory climbed into the back seat.

'And the last thing we want now is another road accident,' Stan remarked as he inserted the key into the ignition and adjusted the driver's seat.

Mallory dozed in the back, the movement and drone of the car's engine lulling her senses.

'Here you are, Mal. Home sweet home.' Stan climbed out and opened the door for her. 'Now straight to bed. The debriefing can be organised for later this afternoon when we've *all* had some sleep.'

'Saturday already?' Mallory asked sleepily as she dug keys from her handbag. 'Say goodbye to Jeremy for me. I feel sorry for you, Stan, to have to live with someone who snores like that.'

Stan chuckled. 'He's a good lad. Off to bed.'

'I can't think of anything I'd like better. Thanks, Stan. For everything.'

Mallory unlocked the door and pushed it open. It seemed a very long time since she'd dressed and left for work that morning—yesterday morning, she corrected herself.

Feeling grimy, Mallory decided to have a quick shower, the hot spray mildly soothing her aching and bruised body. She felt as though she'd been put through the wringer. Towelling herself dry, she slipped on warm baggy PJs and thankfully climbed between her sheets. Her eyes closed the instant her head hit the pillow.

*Would the marriage last? Did Nick and Suzannah stand a chance?*

Mallory wiped at her eyes yet again as she peered out into the bleary, wet and rainy evening.

*How could Suzannah have betrayed her like this? Becoming pregnant and therefore marrying the man that Mallory loved?*

Mallory changed the radio station for the fifth time. Why did everyone have to play love songs? After the wedding, it was the last thing she needed.

She'd just lived through the most humiliating day of her life. Nick's and Suzannah's wedding day.

Mallory had found it difficult to even look at Nick, considering what he'd done to her. She should hate him—and most of her did, but she knew, despite everything, he would always be her one true love.

Her cheek-bones ached from forcing a smile all day long. Watching Suzannah in her shimmering gown of white as she'd laughed and enjoyed herself, it had now finally taken its toll. The tears were silently rolling down her cheeks, much as the rain was steadily pelting the windscreen of her car. It was over now. She would return to Appleton for a few days' rest, before continuing her internship in Sydney.

Mallory switched the radio off altogether as the light turned green. She pressed her foot carefully down on the accelerator.

*WHAM!*

The force of the car that slammed into hers had an instant effect. Mallory felt immense pain down the right-hand side of her body as her car skidded sideways across the road, the rain turning the tar as sleek and smooth as an ice rink.

Then the car began to spin. Once…twice… A lamppost seemed to come out of nowhere as it buckled from the impact of her car hitting it before it landed on the roof. The cave-in knocked her on the head as she spun for the last time, the left-hand side of her car colliding with another stationary car parked nearby.

Feeling as though she were stuck in a sardine can, Mallory looked down at her dress. The beautiful, hot-pink, frilly creation Suzannah had begged her to wear, even though the colour didn't suit her, was now splattered with bright red blood.

The sight made Mallory feel faint.

Get hold of yourself, she ordered. You're an intern. You've seen dead bodies and patients in far worse conditions than this.

Her pep talk was to no avail. Feeling the small amount of food she'd managed to keep down at the wedding reception begin to rise, Mallory vomited before the black void of unconsciousness finally claimed her.

Mallory sat bolt upright in bed, her body bathed in sweat and trembling with fear. Slowly she managed to calm her breathing as she climbed from the sheets and walked out into the kitchen to get a cool glass of water. The clock indicated it was almost three a.m. She'd only been asleep for just over an hour.

Sitting down at her kitchen table, she concentrated on deep-breathing exercises. It had been years since she'd had a terrible nightmare about her car accident. She shouldn't be surprised, considering the retrieval she'd just been through.

Mallory had been trapped for almost seven hours before they'd finally managed to cut her free and transfer her to the Brisbane hospital where she'd trained as a medical student.

She hadn't minded, when she'd finally regained full consciousness, that they'd had to cut and tear the pretty dress from her body in order to tend her wounds. That was how she'd felt. Cut and bruised on the outside, her heart torn to pieces on the inside.

Nick had married Suzannah. Nick had no longer been hers.

Mallory had been repressing her emotions for so long that in the past few weeks since Nick had reappeared in her life *everything* had been pushed to the back of her mind… The situation with Suzannah and the possibility that she herself had been deceived for all those years. Her renewed and passionate feelings for Nick and the nurturing love she felt for his daughter. Her uncertainty at exactly what he wanted from her.

And tonight…the accident, which had triggered her own nightmares once more. It was all too much.

Rising, Mallory went to the cupboard where she stored her medical kit and took some paracetamol to help with the ache that was pounding in her head.

*Thump. Thump. Thump.*

It was getting louder, she thought as she swallowed the tablets. The pounding started again and she realised someone was at the door.

'Mallory!' Nick's voice called, and she immediately shushed him. He'd wake her neighbours. 'Mallory. Open the door.'

'I'm coming,' she called impatiently, and quickly opened the door.

Nick burst past her into the room.

'Why don't you come in, Nick?' she suggested dryly, and closed the door. When he just stood there, fuming, in the middle of the hallway, Mallory shook her head and walked back into the kitchen.

'Would you like a drink?'

'I get out of Theatre, weary and tired…'

When he didn't answer her question, Mallory sat down and crossed her arms over her chest. Nicholas obviously had something to get off his chest—and she had a feeling she wasn't going to like it.

'To find police Sergeant Ryan at the hospital with his full report.' Nick paced up and down the kitchen as he spoke, Mallory's eyes following him. 'I inform him that it's hospital policy to conduct the debriefing at a later time and he tells me he won't be available—he has to get back to his own beat. I say, fair enough.'

'He then sits down and goes through his report with me and wonders why I almost leap from my seat when he reads that the car shifted, the tree branches gave way, the vehicle was now suspended by the Country Fire Services cables and that Dr Newman was in the car at the time!' His voice had risen to yelling point near the end.

'Nick, please, sit down. Calm down. Let me make you some tea.'

'I don't want any damn tea, Mallory. I want to know what you were doing in that car again.' He thumped his fist on the table.

Mallory stared at him for a moment, taking a deep breath while forcing her own emotions to stay calm. 'Rescuing a patient.'

'I thought I told you to leave that to the CFS. There was absolutely no need for you to go back down there and put your life in further jeopardy.'

'Yes, you did…*suggest* that I not go back down. I ignored you.'

'You—' He broke off and spread his arms wide. 'You could have been killed.'

'But I wasn't,' she pointed out, the ache in her head now ready to explode. 'Can't we talk about this at some other time? We've both had an extremely tiring night and—'

'I don't care what time it is.' His voice began to rise again. 'You don't seem to understand your responsibilities here. As head of the retrieval team, it is up to you to make sure no one, *yourself included*, takes unnecessary risks. You wouldn't have allowed anyone else from your team to get into that car, would you?'

'No,' she replied, and was going to say more but Nick cut her off.

'Exactly. Yet you're intent on pursuing these unsafe alternatives. You leave me no option but to request you be removed as head of the retrieval team.'

Mallory had tried to remain calm. She had tried to calm Nick down and had allowed for the fact that he'd been tied up in Theatre for the past six to seven hours, thereby making him extremely fatigued. But now he'd gone too far.

Mallory rose slowly to her feet, her hands clenched into fists at her side. 'Get out,' she told him.

'No.'

'Leave, Nicholas. *Now!*'

He rounded to where she stood with a few strides and placed his hands on her shoulders. 'I'm not leaving.' His grip tightened. 'Not until you see reason. You might have been killed!'

'I *wasn't.*' Mallory broke free from his grasp and walked away. 'I realise that you're angry, Nick, but that gives you no right to come bursting in here in the middle of the night. If you're so intent on pursuing this course of action—removing me as head of the retrieval team—then it's a wonder you told me at all. Why not just do it? It's the way you've done things in the past.'

'Don't start slinging dirty laundry at me, Mallory. Now is not the time or the place to even *begin* to talk about the past. What matters right at this moment...' Nick stabbed his index finger on the table for emphasis '...Is that you behaved irresponsibly and unprofessionally tonight.'

'What? I did nothing of the sort. I did my job,' she yelled back at him.

'I told you not to go back down.'

'You don't seem to understand, Nick. *You* had no say in

what went on tonight. *I* was calling the shots and I think *that's* the part you don't like. The great Nicholas Sterling, not in control of such a delicate situation. You had to sit back and wait until your patient was brought to you. I know you're a man of action, Nick. I know you hate to sit around, but that doesn't give you the right to vent your anger and frustration on me.'

'You're the one who doesn't seem to understand, Mallory. You risked your life.'

'Nine times out of ten that's what retrieval is all about. I have a good team—I have the best team. We've worked together for years and can anticipate each other's movements, without having to say a word, and that's the way it ought to be.'

'I appreciate that but still—you shouldn't have taken the team back down. There was nothing you could do for the patient.'

'You have no say in that decision. You hadn't been down there. You hadn't seen the position of the patient. You had only listened in to what was reported by the various people. For your information, Nicholas, I discussed it with the team—with Jeremy and Stan—about returning back down to be with Tom when he was finally cut free from the wreckage. I voiced your suggestion that we wait and let the CFS do it but after discussion, it was decided—unanimously—that we go back down.

'As to why I was the one in the car, simply because I am the smallest and lightest. My height and weight were on a par with Gail's and it indeed would have been suicide for anyone else to attempt it.

'It wasn't my weight or presence in the car that shifted it—it was when Tom was released from the restraint of his seat belt. Yes it scared me.' She clutched her hand to her heart for emphasis. 'Yes it made me wonder whether this had been the right thing to do but there really was no other alternative. Those CFS guys would not have been able to rescue Tom without our help. Without us there—without the retrieval team—Tom would have died. The CFS would have cut him out but he would have been dead once he'd reached the top. Which was why—as a team—we decided to go back down.'

Nick was silent for a moment. He hadn't moved while she'd spoken except for crossing his arms over his chest—defensively.

'To tell you the truth, Nick, I'm a little hurt that you would think I would take such an enormous responsibility so lightly. Don't you know me well enough by now? I would never risk another team member's life. We always discuss our plans of action and everyone has input but when it comes down to crunch time, yes, I make the final and sometimes terribly difficult decisions, but that's only after intense discussion with the rest of the team.'

'I apologise if you feel I misjudged you,' Nick replied after a moment, his voice more calm than before.

'Thank you.'

'I wasn't implying that you weren't careful, Mal.' He raked a hand through his hair and slumped down into a chair. Mallory came over and sat next to him. 'I just freaked when I found out you were in that car.'

Nick reached out and took her hands in his. 'I have all the confidence in the world regarding your professional and medical abilities. I was worried about your mental state. When I heard how crushed and trapped the patients were, it made me think about your own accident.'

A shudder ripped through him. 'Suzannah told me you were trapped in the car for almost seven hours. Is that true?'

'Yes.'

Nick shook his head in disbelief. 'On the night of my wedding, there you were, almost killed in a car accident.'

Mallory broke her hands free from his and stood. 'I'd

rather not talk about it now, Nick,' she said and crossed to the sink to fill her glass with water. She had never discussed the accident with Nick but obviously Suzannah had. Mallory was thankful now that Suzannah had insisted on hearing as little about the accident as possible. She had hated all the 'blood and gore' stories that went hand in hand with any 'medical stuff'.

'Tonight's accident brought all the memories back, didn't it?' he asked softly, and came to stand behind her. He placed his hands on her shoulders again but this time they were tender and gentle.

Slowly Nick turned her around to face him. He looked deep into her eyes, before scanning her face. 'You've had a nightmare.' It was a statement but Mallory nodded all the same.

'I usually do have nightmares after we attend car accidents.'

'This has happened before?' Nick didn't wait for an answer and crushed her to his chest, his arms holding her protectively. 'Mallory,' he whispered after a moment, 'why do you continue to put yourself through this torture? Leave the retrieval team.'

'I can't.' Mallory pulled back to look at him, happy that he still kept his arms protectively about her. 'Nick, I think back to the team who worked so diligently to get me out of my own car. I owe them my life.'

'But it's all part of their job. You know that.'

'Yes, I do, and I promised myself that once I was qualified I, too, would join a retrieval team. It's my way of saying thank you to the people who rescued me. I may have nightmares from time to time and I accept that, but they also help to remind me exactly why I'm doing this in the first place. Those people were my lifeline. There were so many times when I really couldn't be bothered to fight. I wanted to die, Nick.'

'Don't say that,' he implored.

'It's true. I'd lost you. The man I loved. You were married to my best friend and I had no idea how I would cope, knowing that Suzannah would want to keep in close contact with me—telling me all about your wonderful life together.'

She felt Nick go rigid at her words but his arms remained firmly around her.

'Then I realised that if I let go—if I gave up—those people who had worked so hard, for so long in their rescue attempts would all feel it was their fault. I wasn't going to be responsible for that so I held on. I fought and I won.'

Tears were slowly rolling down Mallory's cheeks as she spoke, and when she'd finished Nick gently wiped them away. Lowering his head, he claimed her lips gently with his, before enfolding her to him once more.

'I can't even begin to imagine what you've been through during the past five years but, as I said before, now is not the time or the place.'

They stood, locked together, in an embrace, each drawing strength from the other. When the clock on the wall chimed half past three Nick looked down at Mallory.

'It's time we got some sleep.' Even as he spoke, he yawned. 'I'm exhausted.'

'That makes two of us.' Mallory hesitated, but only for a fraction of a second, before stepping back and tugging on his hand. 'Come on.'

'Where?'

'To bed.'

'Mallory!' Nick's voice held a hint of surprise as he yawned again.

'I mean so that we can sleep. I'm too tired and so are you.' She led him down the corridor and into her bedroom. 'Just hold me, Nick,' she whispered as the darkness of the room settled over them. 'Like you used to.'

Mallory climbed under the covers and waited for Nick to join her. He kept his trousers on and she was grateful. He really did understand that for tonight all she needed was his arms, comforting and holding her. Washing away the past and the nightmares that lived there.

Snuggling deeper under the covers, Mallory closed her eyes. The warmth of Nick's chest against her back was everything she remembered.

This was where she truly belonged. This was where nothing bad could ever touch her. With Nick at her side, Mallory felt as though she could conquer the world.

# CHAPTER EIGHT

MALLORY stirred lazily and opened her eyes, then allowed them to focus on her beside clock.

'Half past twelve?' she exclaimed as she threw back the covers and scrambled out. Stopping for a moment, she recalled the previous night's events and quickly turned to look at her bed. Nick wasn't there.

'Nick?' she called as she softly padded out to the kitchen. No answer. 'Nick?' she called again, a little louder this time. Still no reply. A quick tour of the house confirmed the fact that Nick wasn't about. Had he even *been* there?

Mallory went through the motions of making coffee and then sat down at the kitchen table to rethink the events leading up to her going to bed. She was positive Nick had come by. That he'd cradled her in his arms ever so sweetly, stroking her hair until she'd fallen into a deep and wonderful sleep.

She almost jumped out of her skin when the phone rang. Quickly snatching up the receiver to stop the loud ringing, she tried to smother a yawn as she said, 'Dr Newman.'

'What time would you like the debriefing to start?'

At the sound of Nick's voice Mallory's heart went into overdrive. She stretched the phone cord so she could sit down, realising her knees were about to give way.

'Hi.' Mallory tried to concentrate on his words but all she could wonder was whether she'd dreamed of him being in her bed. How could she ask him? If she *had* dreamed it, she knew Nick would tease her about it. Could she allow herself to look so... silly?

'Um…' She cleared her throat and tried again. 'Nick…um… What…what was the question?'

When he repeated the question, Mallory heard the smile in his voice. 'What time do you want to schedule the debriefing?'

'Ah…how about four o'clock?'

'Fine. Tom and Gail are still on the critical list but should stabilise soon.'

'Good,' she replied, unable to believe she hadn't even asked about them. What kind of doctor was she?

There was silence on both ends of the line and Mallory began to feel uncomfortable. She needed to find out whether or not Nick had been here earlier that morning. After taking another sip of her coffee, she came up with an innocuous statement.

'You left early.' Hopefully he wouldn't be sure whether she was talking about leaving the hospital in the small hours or her home.

'I needed to get home to Rebekah. Much as I'd have loved to have stayed and held you, I have certain responsibilities that go with being a single parent.'

Mallory let out a sigh of relief. She hadn't imagined it. The warm, tender look in his eyes. The way his fingers had gently caressed her hair. The feel of his strong, protective arms around her.

'Of course. Rebekah must come first.'

'Good. I'll see you at four, then. By the way,' he added. 'You'll find your car has been returned.' Without another word he rang off. Mallory frowned at the receiver for a while, before standing to replace it. She'd forgotten about her car. He hadn't even given her the opportunity to thank him and probaby Arlene, too, for driving it back. Checking the clock again, she realised that fifteen minutes had passed and if she didn't hurry up she'd never get her house calls done.

*     *     *

'Why didn't you call me?' Mallory asked Chloe Hone as she put her medical bag down on the table, pulled out her otoscope and attached a speculum to it.

'I'd heard about that terrible accident last night and knew you'd be around today so I didn't see the point in troubling you further.'

'Don't let it happen again. If I'd known, I'd have been here a lot sooner.'

'Forget to set your alarm?' Chloe asked as she walked around the room, trying to settle little Nathan's cries.

'You could say that. Right, bring him here and let's have a look at that ear.' Mallory showed Chloe how to hold her four-week-old son so that she could effectively take a look at the baby's ear.

'I know, sweetie,' she crooned as he cried more loudly. 'I know it hurts. Just stay still for a little bit longer.' Mallory closed one eye and peered into Nathan's right ear. 'How has he been feeding?'

'He won't settle to feed on the left side but the right side is fine.'

'Temperature?'

'Mild one.'

'Vomiting?'

'Just before you arrived. That's the first time,' Chloe added.

'When I saw him last weekend he was a bit snuffly. That seems to have cleared up, but I'd say the infection has moved to his ears.' Mallory pulled away and kissed little Nathan's head. 'Oh, you poor little thing. I know it's not nice when someone wants to poke and prod where you're sore but I need to.' She kissed his head again. 'Turn him around and hold his head and hands in the same way while I check the other ear,' Mallory instructed.

'This one's fine,' she said a moment later. 'His right ear

is slightly infected. If you'd left it for a few more days, it would have spread to the other ear as well.'

'What's the treatment?'

'I'll prescribe an antibiotic that comes in a syrup mixture, which you can get from the pharmacy.'

Chloe settled Nathan for a feed so that he was lying on his left ear, and the sudden quiet of the room made both women smile.

'The way to a man's heart is definitely through his stomach.' Chloe laughed.

'Now that we have a bit of peace and quiet, I'll explain what's wrong with his ear. It's what we term acute otitis media. It's when there's inflammation in the lining of the middle-ear cleft. When I look into his ear the drum looks red and is slightly bulging, which indicates infection.

'That's probably why he hasn't been sleeping so well and has been tugging on his ears. Give him some infant paracetamol for the pain as well. The antibiotic needs to be given until it's all gone. The amount of syrup you'll receive usually lasts for seven to ten days. If you don't see any improvement within the first three days, you must let me know immediately.'

'I will.'

'Now that he's settled, tell me how *you* are feeling.'

'Sleep-deprived, exhausted, wrung out.' Chloe smiled. 'And it's all worth it in the end. I love my family.'

'Let's have a cuppa and relax,' Mallory suggested.

'Sounds like a good prescription to me.'

Mallory found her way around Chloe's kitchen and made the tea. 'Where's the rest of your brood?'

'Damian's taken them shopping. He was hoping I'd have some time to rest.'

'Then let's make sure you get it.' Mallory pressed a pre-programmed button on her mobile phone which connected her with the pharmacy. She ordered Nathan's antibiotic and asked for it to be delivered.

'I'll bring the paperwork by on my way to the hospital, Reg.'

'No problem, Mallory. I'll get it organised,' the pharmacist told her, and she rang off.

'So…how are things with Nicholas Sterling?' Chloe asked, an enormous smile on her face.

'Why?' Mallory was cautious. 'What have you heard?'

'That you two are an item—again! When was the first time? We've only been here for two years so I've never met the famous Mr Sterling.'

'We…' Mallory hesitated, then shrugged her shoulders. It was old news and if Chloe didn't hear it from her, she'd hear it from someone else. 'We dated five years ago.'

'What happened? Why did you break up?'

Mallory shrugged again, trying to be nonchalant. 'He married my best friend and moved to Brisbane.'

'I'd heard he was a widower.' Chloe nodded and then smiled again at Mallory. 'All the better for you. Now the two of you can pick up where you left off.'

'Or something like that,' Mallory replied with an ironic laugh. 'We'll see.'

'Let the past be the past, Mallory.' Chloe's tone was soft and caring.

'I'm trying but there are just a few more things that need to be clarified.'

'Well, I'm sure everything will come out roses in the end.'

'I certainly hope you're right, Chloe.' Mallory looked at the sleeping baby. 'Nathan seems happier now.' She watched as Chloe bent her head to kiss him. 'He's gorgeous, Chloe.' The words were said in a whisper as emotion choked her vocal cords.

'I'll go and put him down in his cot.'

As Chloe walked out of the room, with little Nathan cradled in her arms, Mallory lifted her own arms into a similar position, imagining what it could possibly be like to hold your own child so lovingly.

She'd held other babies, delivered babies, but never would she know the sensations that Chloe Hone was now feeling. Chloe might be physically exhausted but she was ecstatically happy with her doting husband and three beautiful children.

Mallory felt her eyes prick with tears and quickly brushed them away, repressing her emotions. At least, she rationalised, Chloe appreciated her family. Many women didn't.

When Chloe returned, Mallory had herself under control and was able to conduct the postnatal check with professionalism.

'Now that we have all the medical check-ups out of the way, you go and rest while you can.' Mallory proceeded to pack her medical bag. 'If Nathan wakes, give him some paracetamol, and hopefully by then the antibiotic should be here. You call me if anything bothers you. Ears are very sensitive and can often be a warning sign that something else might be wrong. At this stage I think we have everything under control but if there's the slightest change or if you're not sure about something, you call me. Promise?'

'I promise,' Chloe answered.

'All right. I'll see you next Saturday.' Mallory waved goodbye and climbed into her car. 'Next inquisition to be held by Mrs Jessie McFarland,' she mumbled to herself as she started the engine and went on her way.

'Suzannah was the bad apple in that marriage,' Jessie proclaimed half an hour later. 'Not Nicholas.'

Mallory eyed her patient warily. 'Why haven't you said any of this before?'

'Because it didn't matter before. You're in love with Nicholas Sterling. It's as plain as the nose on your face.'

Mallory was surprised but reasoned that Jessie saw through most people's defences. 'Am I *that* obvious?'

'At least you're not going to deny it. Yes, as a matter of fact, you are that obvious. Just mention the man's name and you get a silly schoolgirl grin on your face, one, I might add, I haven't seen on your face since you *were* a silly schoolgirl.'

'I was twenty-five years old at the time, Jessie. You were married with five children by the time you were twenty-five.'

'We matured a lot faster in those days,' Jessie said. 'What matters now is that you speak to Nicholas and find out *his* side of the story. What really happened all those years ago?'

'I know what happened, Jessie. The more I remember and think about it, the more the hurt returns, and I don't know if it's worth taking another chance with Nick.'

'Which is all the more reason why you *must* talk to him.'

'I love him, Jessie. What if I found it happened just as Suzannah said? What if I find I…can't forgive him? What then?'

'I told you. Suzannah was the wrong one. I'm certain as can be that this is all her doing. You need to hear Nicholas's side of the story as well as the particulars of his marriage to her. It can't possibly be what she led you to believe.'

Mallory was silent for a moment, digesting what Jessie had said. 'I hope you're right.'

'Look back at the time you had with Nicholas. Tell me what you remember.'

'I remember him… I remember him being just the same as he is now. He's kind, caring and sensitive, as well as positive and determined. He has the overwhelming arro-

gance that most men, and especially surgeons, have but for
the most part...' she shrugged '...he's just the same old
Nick.'

'Exactly.' Jessie clapped her hands together in triumph.
'You need to talk to him. Promise me you will.'

Mallory nodded. She had known this would happen
sooner or later. Nick had even told her as much the first
night she'd gone to dinner at his place. They'd needed to
talk but until she could believe that Suzannah wasn't the
little angel she'd been led to believe, Nick's words would
never be able to penetrate the hurt and rejection Mallory
had nursed for so many years.

'I promise,' she said firmly.

'Today?' Jessie pushed further.

Mallory nodded. 'Today, if possible.'


'Tom and Gail are now both off the critical list and their
conditions are stable,' Mallory advised the group as she
completed her debriefing. 'Thank you to everyone who
took part. We're a great team.'

'Here, here,' Stan said, and they broke into a round of
applause.

Everyone stayed to chat for a few more minutes. Mallory
was eager to be with Nick. She'd promised Jessie that she'd
speak to him today, and today it would be. Throughout the
entire debriefing she'd made sure that her gaze had rarely
come into contact with his. The few times it had, it had left
Mallory feeling nervous with tingling anticipation. She'd
needed to concentrate on her words and Nick, just by being
there, had been enough to distract her completely.

She saw him, out of the corner of her eye, rise from his
chair, where he'd been chatting with Kate, and head towards the door.

'Nick... Excuse me, Stan,' she apologised as she'd cut

Stan off in mid-sentence. Nick slowly turned and looked at her, one eyebrow raised questioningly.

'I...' Her throat dried up and she swallowed, before trying again. 'I need to speak to you. Can you wait?'

A brief nod was her only answer and she forced her attention back to Stan. 'Sorry. You were saying?'

'Just that I've noticed such a vast improvement in Jeremy. Every time we go out on a call he impresses me even more than before.'

'You have every reason to be proud of him, Stan. You're the only family he's got and I know you mean the world to him.' Mallory glanced briefly at Nick where he sat at the table, engrossed in some paperwork. Everyone else had left the room. 'Uh...Stan, would you excuse me? I need to see Nick about something.'

'Sure, Mallory.' Stan gave her a wink. 'Shall I put a ''Do Not Disturb'' sign on the door?' He laughed at his own joke as he collected his jacket and keys off the table and left the two of them alone.

Mallory didn't move. She just stood there, on the opposite side of the room to Nick, allowing the silence to envelop her as she watched him. After a few moments he raised his head. His eyes gave nothing away and she wasn't sure whether he was annoyed, nonchalant or simply preoccupied with what he was reading.

'So what do you want to say?' His voice was slightly clipped. Mallory wrung her hands together. She knew she had promised Jessie to talk to him about Suzannah, but now that the moment was actually here Mallory wasn't sure she could go through with it.

When she remained silent he looked away and closed his folder. Then he sat back in his chair and crossed his arms defensively over his chest.

'You're mad at me,' she blurted out, his sudden body language making his feelings clearer.

'And with good reason.'

Mallory stiffened her spine, her defiance coming to the fore. 'May I ask why?'

'Why?' He rose to his feet and slowly pushed in his chair. 'Why? Because we've been in this room for over an hour and not once have you smiled at me—you've barely even looked at me.'

'It was a debriefing,' she justified herself.

'I want to know why you've ignored me. Is it because I left this morning without saying goodbye? Because if it is let me tell you it was damned hard for me to do. You were sleeping so peacefully, like an angel, and after the bad night you'd already had I didn't want to wake you.' Nick raked a hand through his hair in agitation.

'I needed to get home to Rebekah and I thought you understood that. She's my first responsibility and if she were to come into my bedroom—as she does every single morning—and not find me there, she would get very upset. It's only happened once before and that was because I was stuck in Theatre. So as a general rule, I make sure that regardless of what is going on around me, if I have *any* control over events, I'm there when she wakes up. I don't understand why being a considerate and loving father results in you ignoring me.' His voice had risen slightly and she could tell by the way his jaw jutted out that he was defiant on this matter. The only thing was, his entire tirade was unnecessary.

Remaining quiet, Mallory held his gaze for a few more seconds, before quickly crossing to stand before him.

'Nick,' she breathed as she wound her arms around his neck and pulled his head down so their lips could meet. Automatically his arms came to rest at her waist, and when she leaned back to look at him she smiled.

'You are a silly man some days. I completely understand about you leaving this morning. You're right. Rebekah *is* important.' Mallory looked up into the face of the man she loved so deeply and smiled.

'The reason I wouldn't—*couldn't* look at you during the debriefing was because you turn my insides to mush. You've burst back into my life, Nick Sterling, and managed to flip my existence on its axis. Just a single look from you makes my knees grow weak. It makes my heart skip a beat and it makes my palms sweat.'

'Do you realise what you're saying?' he asked.

'Yes.' Mallory's reply was firm and resolute. 'Do you?'

'You love me.' He said the three words with wonder and incredulity.

'I do. I love you, Nicholas Sterling.'

'You love me,' he repeated, and gathered her closer. Crushing her body to his, Nick lowered his head and pressed his lips firmly to hers. 'I can't believe it.' The smile on his face was one of triumph. 'Mallory, you have no idea how I've longed for this moment.' He held her so tightly Mallory thought she might die of asphyxiation.

'Oxygen,' she gasped, and Nick reluctantly let her go.

'Sorry,' he apologised sheepishly as he gazed down into her eyes with adoration. 'You have just made me the happiest of men.'

'I know, Nick, but there's more we need to discuss.'

Nick lowered his head for an instant then looked at her again, his face solemn. 'Suzannah.'

Mallory nodded. 'We need to talk about everything that's happened during the past five years. I know it will be difficult for you—for us—but to move forward we need to understand the past.'

Nick glanced at his watch. 'Why don't we go back to my place? Have some dinner, spend some time with Rebekah and then, when she's asleep, we can talk.'

'All right. Let me go home and change. I'll meet you at your house.'

'You don't need to change,' he protested as his gaze took in her appearance. Her blue denim jeans fitted her perfectly and the white embroidered shirt dressed up the jeans a little. 'You look…incredible to me.' He snagged one of her hands and drew her closer. 'You *are* incredible,' he amended, as his head bent once more to claim her lips.

It was as though they were meant to be together—their mouths knew exactly how to mesh. Nick kissed her soundly with a few short kisses, before cradling her face in his hands and slowly plumbing her senses as his tongue edged its way around the circumference of her mouth. The pressure was slight, almost feathery—something Nick knew drove Mallory to distraction.

Mallory shivered involuntarily and sighed as he finally finished the sweet torture, before deepening the kiss. It was as though he, too, could no longer stand being apart and needed to get to the very centre of her emotional being.

Butterflies churned in her stomach, her knees started to weaken and her palms were definitely moist with perspiration. She was his. She'd known it all along and so had he.

Nick's rough five-o'clock shadow tingled lightly over Mallory's face as he broke free and pressed small kisses all the way around to her ear.

'This is so right,' he whispered. 'We belong together. We've always belonged together.'

It was such an exact replica of her own thoughts that she marvelled at how in tune they were with each other's feelings.

'Let's go to your place first and *then* to mine,' he suggested. 'At least at your place we can be alone with no one to disturb us.'

'Nick.' Mallory pulled away and shook her head with a smile. 'You're incorrigible.'

'What?' His smile was sexy and wild and for an instant

Mallory was very tempted but knew she'd hate herself later. Nothing had been cleared up between them. There was still so much that needed to be said.

Nick exhaled. 'You're right, of course,' he said, as though he were still reading her thoughts. 'But you can't blame a guy for trying. It's just that I love you so damned much, it's hard to keep my hands off you at times.'

Mallory smiled, marvelling at the way the words just rolled off his tongue. He loved her so much. She doubted if she would ever tire of hearing him say it.

'Nick, I'll meet you at your place in half an hour.'

'Make it fifteen minutes,' he suggested, before kissing her briefly again.

'I'll do my best,' she said, still feeling a little shy now her true feelings had been revealed. They exchanged another kiss before she turned and reluctantly left him.

When Nick pulled into his driveway in his Jaguar, his spirits were soaring. There was a spring in his step as he collected his briefcase and went inside the house. Mallory loved him. What more could a man ask for?

The sudden ear-splitting scream pierced his heart. 'Rebekah,' he called urgently, dropping his briefcase on the floor and rushing up the stairs towards her bedroom. 'Rebekah?'

There was no answer. Rebekah knew that whenever he or Arlene called her she was to answer immediately. This time she didn't respond.

Nick hurried into her room, his eyes scanning frantically. The bookshelf had fallen, trapping Rebekah underneath it. Nick's heart hammered in his throat as he quickly bent and began tossing books out of the way before he could successfully remove the wooden shelves.

'Rebekah?' he heard Arlene calling.

'In here,' he called back, and soon the housekeeper was by his side, helping to remove the debris.

'She must have climbed up on the shelves and overbalanced,' he surmised as he was finally able to scoop up and cradle the little unconscious girl in his arms.

'Sweetheart? Rebekah?' he soothed, but received no response. He checked her pupils, took her pulse, made sure she didn't have any cuts or scratches. 'Honey girl, it's Daddy,' he said, and this time her eyes flickered open for a brief second before they closed again. She started to whimper and Nick's heart constricted in pain. He hated it when she suffered.

'Where is it sore, baby? Does your head hurt?' He ran one hand expertly over her fragile little bones. 'We need to get her to the hospital.' He looked up at Arlene who was wringing her hands in anguish. 'Her leg is broken. Get my medical bag from the car and I'll stabilise her leg.'

'Right away.' Arlene's voice choked on a sob. She turned to go but Nick stopped her.

'Get me some paracetamol first. It will help ease the pain.'

Arlene did as he asked and then said, 'I'll get your bag.' Then she rushed out of the room. Nick administered the liquid paracetamol through a dropper.

Rebekah was still whimpering. 'Shh. It's all right, darling. Daddy's here. Everything's going to be fine.' Through the multitude of emotions Nick was experiencing, uppermost in his mind was fear. If anything happened to Rebekah, he...he didn't know what he would do.

Being a father, that meant the world to him. Rebekah was the most perfect thing he'd ever had in his life. Even though his marriage to Suzannah had been a farcical nightmare, Rebekah had been the little ray of sunshine which had brightened his existence.

He was angry at her for attempting to climb up on the

shelves, especially when she'd been told not to do it before. He was angry with himself for not ensuring the shelves were better stabilised. He was thankful he'd been here to deal with the situation. He was cross with himself for having dallied with Mallory. If he hadn't, he'd have been home sooner and Rebekah would have been playing with him, rather than making mischief in her bedroom.

When Arlene returned Nick splinted the leg. 'Let's go.' His tone was brisk, his body rigid, his jaw set.

'You'll have to drive, Arlene. Rebekah may have a head injury and for the moment she's comfortable in my arms, so the less she's moved, the better.'

He knew his housekeeper was concerned about driving his Jaguar, especially as it was so much bigger than her own car, but there was nothing else to be done. To transfer Rebekah over to Arlene could cause more injuries and he was determined that his daughter was going to suffer as little as possible.

He heard the loud blare of a car horn and looked up to find Mallory slowing her car to turn into his driveway.

'Never mind, Arlene. I'll go in Mallory's car. Open the door.'

He watched as the look on Mallory's face turned from one of happiness to one of horror in a matter of seconds as she took in the scene before her.

'What's happened?' She was switching off the engine and getting out of the car.

'Get back in,' he told her briskly but quietly. Raising his voice, that would only have resulted in disturbing his daughter. 'Rebekah needs to go to hospital.'

Mallory didn't ask questions but did as she was told. Arlene shut the car door once Nick and Rebekah were settled. 'Just drive,' he ordered, the child in his arms whimpering again.

'Shh, baby. It's all right. Daddy's here,' he crooned. 'Daddy's here. Daddy will fix everything. Shh.'

# CHAPTER NINE

WHEN they arrived at the hospital they were met by an orderly with a barouche. Mallory had called ahead to let the hospital know of their imminent arrival.

'I need X-rays of her left femur and more importantly, her head.' Nick was giving orders. 'Mallory, I've given her paracetamol but nothing else. Find out the correct dosage for a child of two and get her some analgesics.

'Contact the children's hospital in Brisbane and organise for a paediatric orthopaedic surgeon to come here immediately. The less Rebekah is moved, the better,' Nick instructed, as he walked with the barouche into the hospital and through to X-Ray.

Mallory left them to do his bidding. Analgesics for a two-year-old. She placed a call to Brisbane and spoke with the director of orthopaedics at the children's hospital. Once she had related the particulars and been advised on the correct dosage of pain relief, she asked about a surgeon to come to Appleton to look at the patient.

'I'm sorry, Dr Newman. I can't possible spare anyone today.'

'The patient is Rebekah Sterling. Nicholas Sterling's daughter,' she added hopefully. She knew Nick had friends in high places and at the moment he needed every string available pulled.

She heard the director groan with frustration. 'Is there any sign of head injury?' he asked.

'She's being X-rayed now and has been slipping in and out of consciousness.'

'I don't know what else I can do. Nick is a friend but

I'm sorry, Dr Newman, I can't possibly spare anyone to send to Appleton. Believe me, if I could I would. Best to get her flown down here in the hospital's helicopter and we'll ensure she's seen immediately.'

Mallory sighed and the director picked up on it. 'I know he's not going to like it but it's the best I can do. I'm sorry you'll have to bear the brunt of his wrath over this matter but that's the way it has to be.'

'I'm sure I'll cope,' Mallory said with a small smile in her voice. This man *did* know Nick and she realised his promise of immediate care would be fulfilled. She rang off and then set about organising the helicopter.

Once the transfer details were taken care of she called Arlene.

'Oh, how is she?' Arlene sounded very distressed.

'She's in X-Ray. We'll know more soon.'

'It's my fault. It's all my fault. I was outside, bringing the washing in before it rained, and I should have been watching her. I've told her time and time again not to climb on those bookshelves, that they'd tip over on her... And now... I should have been watching her.' She broke off on a sob.

'Arlene, you can't be expected to watch her twenty-four hours a day,' Mallory told her, the events of the past half hour falling into place. So *that* was how Rebekah had hurt herself. 'Don't be ridiculous. Of course it isn't your fault and I'm sure Nick would agree with me. Children can get into mischief right in front of your nose and still manage to hurt themselves. Don't blame yourself. She'll be as right as rain.' Even as she said the words, Mallory was trying to force herself to believe them. It all depended on that head X-ray. If she'd suffered a concussion, or had fractured her skull, things could take a turn for the worse.

'Oh, Mallory, I hope so. How's Nicholas?'

'Feeling helpless.'

'That's not good.' She hesitated for a moment and then volunteered, 'Mallory—be careful. He's liable to say things he doesn't mean, so if he takes his anger out on you don't pay any attention to what he's actually saying. OK.?'

'I'll try,' Mallory answered. 'What I need for you to do now, Arlene, is pack a bag for both Nick and Rebekah. She's being transferred to Brisbane for further treatment and will, no doubt, be staying for a few nights.'

'Oh, dear.' Arlene sniffed. 'Does she really have to go? Can't someone come here?'

'I've tried my hardest.'

'Did you tell them it was for Nicholas?' she asked imploringly.

'Yes, and I spoke to the director. He can't spare any staff to fly here so Rebekah must go down to Brisbane.'

'Do you think Nick would mind if I came, too?' Arlene asked.

'I'm sure he'd appreciate it. You are Rebekah's grandmother, Arlene.'

'Not by blood,' the housekeeper protested.

'No. By love,' Mallory responded tenderly. 'And that's far more important. Get everything organised and lock the house up. They'll be leaving in about half an hour.'

'Right. I'll be there.'

Mallory rang off and returned to Radiology with the analgesics for Rebekah. She was also interested to see the results of the X-rays.

'What's the situation?' she asked quietly at Nick's side.

He turned and looked at her, his eyes wild. Nick obviously felt helpless. He wasn't here as a surgeon in command, he was here as a father. There was nothing—medically—he could do to help his daughter and it was tearing him apart.

He'd hardly said a word to her on the drive here but

under the circumstances she understood. Rebekah meant the world to him—as she did to Mallory herself.

Seeing him standing outside his home with the small, limp girl in his arms, it had caused an instant panic to ripple through her being. Mallory sent up a silent prayer, hoping that it was just a case of a broken leg. If that was all then Rebekah, in time, would recover.

'Head X-ray shows a small hairline fracture. I want a CT scan performed to rule out any further injury. I'm still waiting on the films for her leg.'

'I have an injection for her.' Mallory set down the sterile kidney dish she'd used to carry everything in. She opened the swab, unwrapped the needle and drew up the shot. Swabbing Rebekah's right thigh, she injected it into the fatty tissue.

'There you are, darling,' Mallory said softly once she'd finished. 'That will help with the pain.'

Rebekah's eyes fluttered open at the sound of her voice. The child looked at her for a minute, quickly scanned the room until she saw Nick and then closed her eyes again.

Mallory felt a lump form in her throat. Rebekah was so vulnerable, so helpless. All Mallory's suppressed maternal instincts came bursting out as she tenderly ran her fingers through the little girl's curls.

'Everything will be all right. Just sleep for now.' Tears sprang into her eyes. So this was how a mother felt when her child was ill. It was devastating, heart wrenching and unbearable. No wonder Nick didn't want to leave her alone. After everything he'd been through in the past, she knew Rebekah was his pride and joy.

She looked up at him, trying to convey that she understood his feelings. He was watching his daughter, his jaw clenched tight.

'When will the surgeon arrive?' he asked.

'She has to go to Brisbane, Nick.'

'No.'

'I spoke with the director of orthopaedics. I told him it was your daughter but he can't spare the staff—not today. He asked for her to be transferred and promised that she'd be seen immediately upon arrival.'

'No,' he reiterated. 'I will not allow her to be moved yet again. She's in too much pain. She needs a CT scan.'

Mallory counted to ten. 'Nick,' she said firmly. 'I understand how you're feeling—'

'You have *no idea* how I'm feeling,' he responded vehemently. 'You're not a mother. You don't have children of your own. How could you possibly understand how I feel? This is my *daughter*, Mallory. My own flesh and blood. She's lying here with a head injury, broken bones, in pain—and there's nothing I can do.' He ground his teeth. Raising his voice, it would only result in distressing Rebekah even more so his words were said carefully but with determination.

He had no idea of the anguish he was causing Mallory. No, Rebekah was not her own flesh and blood. She was Suzannah's. Mallory was unable to have any children of her own but had taken heart in the knowledge that if she loved Rebekah enough, that would be all that mattered. Nick seemed unable to comprehend that even though Rebekah had not come from Mallory's own womb it didn't mean her true feelings were to be doubted. She loved the child, rejoiced in her and needed those childish little smiles to make her life complete.

'If only I'd gone straight home after the debriefing, none of this would have happened.' Nick's words drove yet another blade through her heart. Not only was he attacking her emotions toward Rebekah, he was now discounting them toward himself.

'Nick, you can't blame yourself.' What had transpired after the debriefing had been so very precious to her—the mutual declarations of their love—and here Nick was almost wishing it hadn't happened.

'I *do* blame myself, Mallory. I'm a single father, first and foremost. What business did I have, dilly-dallying with you, when I might have prevented this terrible accident?'

Mallory decided to swallow the hurt he was evoking. He was only venting his anger on her. Arlene had warned her he might do that. She'd advised Mallory to let it wash over her, but it was extremely hard to do.

'I may not be a mother, Nick, but that doesn't mean I don't understand this situation. I love Rebekah as though she were my own. I, too, feel devastatingly helpless, but in this situation you have to do what's best for your daughter. A surgeon can't be spared from the children's hospital in Brisbane. Rebekah *must* go by helicopter down to Brisbane to be treated.'

'You have no right,' he replied coldly.

'I have *every* right,' she told him sternly. 'I'm the admitting doctor. Rebekah is *my* patient. You're her parent—now act like it.' Mallory held Nick's piercing gaze, not allowing herself to be daunted by it. He might hold her heart, he might have said terrible things to her, but it was nothing compared to what he'd done in the past. She knew she'd forgive him—she loved him and once Rebekah was on the road to recovery he'd come to his senses.

'The helicopter leaves in twenty minutes. Arlene is on her way here with clothes for you, herself and Rebekah. You'll be at least three to four days in Brisbane before Rebekah can be transferred back here. I'll ensure your clinics and operating lists are postponed until you return.

'Some more advice, Nick.' Mallory lowered her voice a little but her words were quite serious. 'Don't push the staff around in Brisbane. They may not be as…lenient as I am. Don't insist on observing in Theatre if they need to operate on Rebekah. You know it's against hospital rules. You have a lot of friends there, Nick. Try to keep them.'

'Finished with your...lecture, Dr Newman?' he asked coldly.

'For now.' Mallory continued to hold his gaze.

'So I take it you're not planning on coming to Brisbane with us?' Before she could reply he added, 'Typical. I thought you were different, Mallory. I thought you really cared about Rebekah. *Loved* her.'

'I *do* love her,' Mallory stressed, 'and, of course, I'm coming to Brisbane, but only for the transfer. I'd love to stay with her, Nick, believe me, but I can't. You know my responsibilities here.'

Nick clenched his jaw. 'What about Theatre?' he asked. 'If she needs surgery, will you stay for that? They'll let *you* in.'

Mallory knew what he was getting at. She wasn't a blood relation to Rebekah and would therefore be admitted into Theatre as an observer.

'If they agree, I'll be there. I love her, Nick,' Mallory said more softly, tears brimming in her eyes. 'With all my heart, soul and mind.'

Nick looked down at his little girl. 'She's so helpless, Mal,' he said quietly.

Mallory's heart went out to him. Nick was in no man's land. Rebekah being hurt, it was more than he could bear. In a way she was thankful she'd been the one to bear the brunt of his anger.

'Films are ready,' the radiographer announced as he came into the treatment room.

'Well, put them up so we can have a look,' Nick demanded.

The X-ray viewing box was switched on and the films hooked up.

'A greenstick fracture to the left thigh. As you can see, the bone is bent on one side and splintered on the other.'

'I *know* what a greenstick fracture is, thank you very much.' Nick's tone was harsh. The radiologist looked at Mallory and shrugged his shoulders, before leaving.

'So she will require surgery.' He exhaled slowly as the situation sank in.

'It's minor, Nick, and the operation to realign the splintered part of the bone back into place takes less than thirty minutes. Slap a plaster cast on her leg and she's done.'

Nick looked at her and then down at Rebekah. 'She's never had a general anaesthetic before.' His tone was soft and for the first time since he'd bundled himself and the small child into her car Mallory was talking to the *real* Nick.

'She'll be fine.' Mallory crossed to his side and rested a hand on his shoulder. 'I'll stay with her in Theatre. They'll do the CT scan first but, considering her vital signs are good, I'm sure no further complications will show. The hairline fracture will heal itself with time. I'll be with her all the way.'

Nick looked at her, giving a brief nod. 'Thanks.'

'Is there any family history regarding allergies to general anaesthetics?' Mallory felt compelled to ask.

'Not that I know of.' He shrugged. 'As far as Suzannah's side of the family goes, I know very little of her history.'

'We'll make sure every precaution is taken then. Anaesthetics have drastically improved even in the last five to ten years. She'll be fine, Nick,' Mallory reiterated. '*You'll* be fine. Soon she'll be at home, complaining because she can't run everywhere at the speed of light, like she's used to doing. Rebekah will need a lot of tender, loving care—but she has the perfect father to give it to her.'

Nick reached for her with his free hand, the other one still firmly holding his daughter's. 'Come here,' he urged.

When she was standing before him, Nick bent his head
and pressed his lips firmly to hers. 'I'm sorry,' he whispered. 'I said some awful things to you. Forgive me?'

'Already forgotten,' she replied, and kissed him back.


Rebekah was given a general anaesthetic for the CT scan.
She needed to be absolutely still and the machine was
rather frightening—even for some adults. As Mallory had
predicted, everything was fine, except for that small hairline
fracture which had shown up on the normal X-rays. She
quickly reported the findings to Nick, who visually relaxed
and sank into a chair. He and Arlene were waiting in the
doctors' tealounge in the theatre block.

The next step was to realign Rebekah's leg. Mallory gave
Nick a nod, before turning and walking into Theatre after
the orthopaedic surgeon.

Seeing Rebekah's small body, limp with anaesthesia, almost made her want to weep. It was different when a child
was sleeping—a natural, healthy sleep—rather than being
sedated. She'd seen it on countless occasions with other
patients, but this was Rebekah. This was the little girl
whom she loved as her own, and it nearly broke her heart.
Get a grip, Newman, she instructed herself as the theatre
staff prepared for the operation. It proceeded without a
hitch. Mallory managed to switch off her emotional feelings
and observe the techniques the orthopaedic surgeon used.
She wouldn't have minded becoming a surgeon but knew
that the mundane and often unsung work of her general
practice was definitely for her. She was happy where she
was, and the retrieval team work gave her that thrill which
was often missed in routine medicine.

Finally, the cast was in place and Rebekah was being
wheeled to Recovery. Mallory went with her, holding her
hand as they went.

'Mallory.' Nick appeared at her side, his face anxious with worry.

'She's fine, Nick. The procedure went well, with no complications, and she'll make a complete recovery.'

Mallory released her hold on Rebekah's hand and stepped back, allowing Nick access to his daughter.

'She's really all right.' The statement was made with astonishment, as though he'd expected something terrible to happen.

'She's fine. The surgeon should be out soon and will, no doubt, want to talk to you.' Mallory took a few steps away from Rebekah's bed and Nick looked up at her.

'Where do you think you're going? I want you here— with Rebekah.'

Mallory smiled. 'She's fine, Nick, and she has you. I'm going to tell Arlene the good news. Then I'm going across to the general hospital to check up on Tom and Gail.' She shrugged. 'I'd just like to see how they're progressing.'

'OK. but don't be gone too long. Once Rebekah comes around I'm sure she'll want to see you.'

'"And then my heart with pleasure fills / And dances with the daffodils."' She quoted Wordsworth to him. 'You generally know just the right things to say to a girl, Nicholas Sterling. Saying that Rebekah would want me here is like manna from heaven.'

He reached out his free hand to her and she took it. Tugging her closer, Nick planted a brief kiss on her lips. 'It's true, but not only would Rebekah want you—I want you, too.' He kissed her again a few more times before she slowly pulled away.

'The sooner I go…' She left the sentence hanging and Nick released her.

'Go and tell Arlene that our little girl is fine. I'll try and talk the recovery nurses into letting her come in.'

'I'm sure you will, Nick.' Mallory laughed. He was back. Her lovable, caring and silver-tongued darling was back.

She watched as Arlene's face relaxed and then brightened at the news she brought. After changing from theatre scrubs back into her clothes, Mallory crossed the road to the main hospital, a skip in her step. She was so happy. After the way the day had started out—being up with the retrieval team, having an argument with Nick, house calls, the debriefing and then the incident with Rebekah—she couldn't think of a more fitting end than being as happy as she felt.

She stopped at the small rise in the hill between the hospitals and admired the end of the sunset. Glorious. And she was sure that if he had the power Nick would have created this spectacular sunset just for her.


Tom and Gail were now both stable and holding their own when Mallory went to the intensive care unit. Tom's paraplegia had been confirmed and she knew that his road to recovery was going to be long and hard.

Gail's internal injuries would also heal in time but she didn't envy the terrifying nightmares which she knew, would live with both of them for the rest of their lives. She knew—from personal experience.

Both patients were sedated but she read up on their charts, glad that they'd made it through. The small glow of satisfaction in a job well done settled within her heart as she started to walk out of the ward.

'Dr Newman?'

Mallory turned around. A tall, elderly man was walking towards her. 'Excuse me, are you Dr Newman?' He had a grey moustache and his face was drawn with worry. He cleared his throat, his honey-coloured eyes, piercing her soul.

'Yes. Can I help you?'

'You can shake my hand.' He extended his hand and Mallory took it. He shook hers heartily. 'I'm Winston Camerons—Gail's father.'

'I see.' Mallory's smile increased. 'She's making a good recovery.'

'It's thanks to you and your team. From what the staff here have told me, your medical retrieval team were the ones to get her out.'

'We were, Mr Camerons, along with the CFS and police, but all in all we have a very special team and we were glad we could help your daughter.'

'If you don't mind me asking, Dr Newman…' He hesitated for a moment. 'Why do you do it? Why do you put your own life in danger to save others?'

'Because other people did it for me, Mr Camerons. I was in a terrible accident many years ago and actually suffered similar injuries to your daughter. She'll be fine, Mr Camerons. As long as she has the love and support of those around her, she'll get through this ordeal.'

'Young Tom's not been so lucky. They told me he won't walk again. We've known the family since before either of the children were born.'

'Tom has a lot of issues he'll need to face but, as his friends, I hope you'll help him to realise that he's still alive. I'm sure once he finds out he'll never walk again that he'll feel his life is over, but it isn't. Believe me, there were some touch-and-go times and for a few moments it didn't look as though he'd make it. But he did. It wasn't his time to die. I hope one day, he'll realise that.'

Mr Camerons was silent for a while, absorbing what Mallory had said. 'Thank you again,' he said and this time there were tears glistening in his eyes. 'I mean it. Please, pass on my thanks to everyone involved in saving our children's lives.'

'It was our...pleasure. I'm in Appleton, Mr Camerons. Stop by and see me some time.'

'That we will do, Dr Newman. You can count on it.'

Mallory made her way slowly back to the children's hospital, knowing it was probably time she headed back to Appleton. It wouldn't do for the town to be without its doctor. Nick and Arlene would be staying behind with Rebekah.

'Hopefully,' Nick said to her a while later as she bent over to kiss Rebekah's forehead, 'we can transfer her back to Appleton tomorrow some time.' Rebekah had been moved to her own room and Arlene was sitting, knitting, in the corner, keeping watch with Nick.

'Children do tend to recover so much quicker than adults,' Mallory agreed. 'You take care, Nicholas. Don't go skipping meals or sleep. You won't do Rebekah any good if you do. Doctor's orders.' She pointed her index finger at him for emphasis.

'You're not my doctor,' he replied as he released his hold on Rebekah's hand and placed his arm about Mallory's waist. 'You're my fiancée.'

Mallory raised her eyebrows in surprise and then looked across at Arlene who had stopped her knitting. 'Did you hear that, Arlene? I'm supposedly Nick's fiancée.'

'Yes.' The older woman's lips twitched as she tried to hide a smile. 'I heard what he said.' Arlene went back to her knitting.

'Forgive me for pointing out a small flaw in your thought process, Nick, but you haven't actually *asked* me to marry you. So how could I possibly be your...fiancée?'

'A small oversight.' He shrugged. 'I had planned to ask you today.'

'Oh, when was that?' Mallory teased. 'When you showed up on my doorstep in the wee hours to argue with me? Or when you got mad at me after the debriefing? Or when you were ranting and raving earlier back at Appleton General Hospital?'

'OK.' Nick withdrew his arm from around her waist and shoved his hands in his pockets, his body language screaming his defensiveness. 'It hasn't worked out as I planned. The fact of the matter is that I *do* want to marry you, Mallory. So, what do you say?'

'That's it? That's my proposal?' she asked incredulously.

'Well, it's not exactly the way I planned it,' Nick responded.

'Good, because I don't accept that proposal. Besides,' she reminded him, all humour gone from her voice, 'we have a few things to discuss before any proposal scene can take place.'

'You're right,' he agreed. 'Regardless, I'll walk you out to the helicopter. Arlene, keep an eye on our girl.'

'Goodbye, Mallory.' Arlene stopped knitting and stood up. 'Thank you for everything.' And then, surprising Mallory further, the other woman embraced her.

Mallory returned the hug and only barely did she hear Arlene whisper in her ear, 'Make sure you give him a bit of a run-around, before accepting. He deserves it.'

Mallory smiled warmly back at her new-found conspirator and nodded. 'See you—hopefully, sooner rather than later.'

'Take care,' Arlene instructed.

'What was all that about?' Nick asked as they walked down the ward and into a long corridor.

'What?'

'Arlene. She rarely takes to anyone she hasn't know since birth, but with you, Mallory, she treats you as the daughter she never had.'

'And I count that as a privilege.'

'You're amazing, do you know that?'

'Nope, but I'm counting on you to tell me.'

Nick laughed and draped his arm around her shoulders. 'I know we have a lot of things to discuss, but I'm sure we can do it, Mallory. I know we'll get there. You love me, I love you. Everything else is…irrelevant.'

They stopped by the lifts and Mallory pressed the button to summon one. She looked down at her hands, not wanting this day to finish on a sad note. How on earth was she going to tell Nick that she couldn't have children? Would his love for her be enough to get them through?

'Nick… I—'

'Shh.' He bent his head and placed his lips briefly on hers. 'It can wait. Everything will be fine—trust me.'

Mallory nodded as a lift stopped in front of them and the doors whooshed open. They stepped in and pressed the button for the top floor. Only this specific bank of lifts took them to the rooftop which was where the helipad was located.

When they stepped outside a cool breeze whisked around them. Now that the sun had set, the evening would become rather cool. Floodlights lit the area and the helicopter pilot gave Mallory the thumbs-up when he saw her. He proceeded with his pre-flight check and she took the opportunity to say a proper goodbye to Nick.

'Call me tomorrow,' she instructed. 'Please, keep me up to date with any change, good or bad, in Rebekah's treatment.'

'Will do,' he promised, both arms sliding around her waist as he drew her close to his body. 'You take care, Dr Newman. We'll have that talk as soon as we can so that the wedding preparations can be made and nights apart will no longer be acceptable.'

'Nick,' she protested again with a smile, but he simply lowered his head and captured her lips with his.

The kiss was soft and gentle yet filled with promise. The warm, masculine scent of him swirled throughout Mallory's body and she sighed with relief. As the wind began to pick up slightly, Nick gathered her closer, protecting and shielding her from its coolness.

Mallory's heart pounded with love for him and the knowledge that her feelings were reciprocated only intensified her own. Nick loved her. That was all that mattered and, hopefully, when he learned the truth it would be all they needed.

# CHAPTER TEN

'DOES Nick love you?' Jessie McFarland asked the next day.

Mallory had needed to talk to someone and Jessie was the best listener in town. Besides, she trusted Jessie's opinion, which was what she was seeking now.

'He says he does.' Mallory looked down at her hands and hesitated. Then she raised her eyes and met Jessie's fair and square. 'He says he wants to get married but he knows we need to talk about the past before we can secure our future.'

'Then talk to him,' Jessie urged. 'I don't know. You young people nowadays need to have a major crisis before you start to actually work things out. In my day we always had the threat of war and so we never wasted a single, precious moment of the time we had together. At least...' she shrugged '...that was the way *I* lived and I taught all my kids the same.'

'I will talk to him—about Suzannah—but...'

'Well, go on, child—out with it.'

'There's more.' Mallory stood and began walking up and down Jessie's front porch where they were enjoying a cup of tea. 'Remember that accident I had all those years ago?'

'Yes. Terrible it was. What of it?'

'Well...' Mallory took a deep breath. She'd never told anyone about this. Not even her family. 'This is so hard for me to say,' she mumbled.

'Just say it.' Jessie's voice was calm and soothing. 'You know I love you, Mallory. I've told you so before. I also

know that I don't need to hear what you're about to say.
I'm listening because I feel *you* need to *say* it.'

'You're right. I do need to say it.' She paused for a
moment, then began. 'In that accident I sustained terrible
injuries to my pelvis and, well…' She took another breath
and then blurted, 'I can't have children.'

Jessie was silent, her gaze never leaving Mallory's face.
'That must be hard for you to handle.'

'It is. It's always wrenched at me cruelly but, Jessie, I'm
hoping that when I tell Nick he'll realise that Rebekah is
enough for us. Do you think he will? Do you think he'll
still accept me, knowing I can never bear him another
child? One of our own flesh and blood? Don't get me
wrong,' Mallory added quickly. 'I love Rebekah as though
she *were* my own. From what I've heard, Suzannah never
loved her so the little girl is just waiting to be loved by a
mother figure. I want to be that person but once Nick learns
about this…this…condition I have, will it force him to re-
ject me?'

'Does he *want* more children?'

'Yes.' Mallory hung her head dejectedly. 'Yes, he does.
He's such a wonderful father—he deserves to have a whole
gaggle of children.'

'He loves you, Mallory, and you love him. You have
Rebekah, as you've already pointed out, and perhaps that
will be enough.'

Mallory slumped back down into her chair and buried
her face in her hands. 'Oh, Jessie. How on earth am I going
to tell him?'


'Mallory.' She heard Nick call her as she walked out of the
clinic and into the car park. It was just after six o'clock on
Friday night and she'd had a very hectic clinic. She didn't
have the strength to face Nick—not yet.

Fumbling with her keys, she willed the correct key to

present itself, but it refused. Why was it that whenever she was in a hurry she could never find the right key?

'Mallory.' His voice was closer now but she concentrated on finding the key.

'Got it,' she mumbled, and quickly unlocked her car door.

'Mallory.' Nick came to stand behind her and, placing his hands on her shoulders, gently turned her around to face him.

'I was going to ask you if you've been avoiding me on purpose but I think I've just discovered the answer for myself. My next question is—why?'

'I…I've been busy,' she muttered, unable to meet his gaze.

'Mallory.' Nick placed his hand under her chin and lifted her head so she was forced to look at him. 'You're a rotten liar. When Rebekah was transferred to Appleton General you were there at least twice a day to see her. Since she's been discharged you've visited daily, but each time I've somehow managed to miss you.'

Mallory shrugged but found that her tongue seemed to be tied in a knot and was refusing to work. Throughout her week of self-imposed exile from Nick she'd almost forgotten how incredibly handsome he was—almost, but not quite. She'd needed just a bit more time to get her thoughts straight, to figure out *what* she was going to tell him about Suzannah and *how* she was going to tell him she couldn't have children. It had kept her awake at night, the only bright spots in her day being her visits with Rebekah.

Now, as she looked into his deep blue eyes, she felt all coherent thought leave her. She loved him so much—she hurt to be without him. Yet the thought of losing him for ever had made her procrastinate during the past week.

'We need to talk, Mallory. There's quite a bit of baggage

from our past that we need to rid ourselves of before announcing our engagement.'

'Aren't you jumping the gun just a little bit, Nick?' she asked. 'As far as I can recall, you've never asked me to marry you,' she pointed out, glad that her senses appeared to be working again.

He eyed her for a second. 'Is *that* what's bothering you? The fact that I haven't proposed properly to you? Because, if it is, let me just set your mind to rest. When I propose, Mallory, you'll be in no doubt as to what is truly happening.'

Nick bent his head and kissed her briefly. He looked down into her eyes as she murmured, 'I've missed you, Nick. Kiss me again. *Please*, kiss me.'

'As you wish,' Nick replied, gathering her closer.

She must have been a fool, she thought as his lips moved warmly over her own, to have thought that she could live without him—especially after all they'd been through in the past. No. Nick was hers.

His tongue entered her mouth with a raw and passionate hunger she'd yearned for in the past week. Mallory's hunger matched his as the kiss intensified. Nick pushed her roughly against her car, leaning against her and smothering her body with his.

They couldn't get close enough to allow their true feelings to be displayed—the extent of their love for one another.

'Nick,' she gasped as his teeth nipped her bottom lip. 'Nick, I'm on fire. I want you.' She plunged her fingers into his hair and kissed him back with ardent desire. 'I need you.' She breathed the words between their lips, involving every sense throughout her body in the display of her feelings.

A few moments later she pulled back and framed his face with her hands. 'I love you, Nicholas Fitzwilliam Sterling.'

A smile tugged at her swollen lips as she said his middle name.

'It's going to amuse you for the rest of your life, isn't it?' he groaned, and shook his head. 'Are you free now? Before you answer that, I think I should warn you that if you say no I won't believe you.'

Mallory's smile was full of promise. 'No,' she teased, and Nick groaned.

'Are you serious or not?'

'I'm always serious when it comes to you, my darling,' she whispered. 'Yes, I'm free. How about you? Are *you* free?'

'I made sure I was. I didn't care whether you'd planned to avoid me for the rest of your life, I was at the end of my rope and was going to take matters into my own hands whether you liked it or not. But, considering your some-what…open display of affection just now, I'm happy to see that you're at least willing to negotiate. Although I can think of a better location than in the clinic car park where the entire main street can see us.'

Mallory lowered her gaze and then looked up at him, all traces of laughter gone from her face. 'What if we can't accept the past, Nick? What if it jeopardises our future?'

Nick cradled her in his arms, resting her head against his chest. 'We have to get over it, Mal. There's no other alternative if we want to spend the rest of our lives together.'

'Get in,' Mallory instructed. 'It is time to put the past to rest—once and for all.' If she didn't do it now, she'd end up running from him again until the courage she'd been searching for all week showed up.

'Where do you want to go?' Nick asked as he came around to the passenger side of her car.

'My house. No one will disturb us there.'

'Unless there's an emergency,' he added.

'Let's pray there isn't.' Mallory sighed.

Neither of them said much on the drive to Mallory's house, although Nick's hand remained on her knee throughout the trip.

When they arrived Nick held her hand, allowing her to unlock the door but claiming it back once again. It was as though he'd never let her go—regardless of what happened.

'Would you like a drink? Tea? Coffee?' Mallory asked, feeling very uncomfortable. Both of them knew they had to discuss Suzannah, but where on earth were they supposed to start?

'No, thanks, Mal. I think we should get down to business. Let's get Suzannah Martel and all her devious works out into the open and clear the air between us—once and for all.'

He guided her over to the comfortable lounge chairs and urged her to sit. Finally, he released her hand, but not before bringing it to his lips. 'Remember, throughout this, that I love you. I always have.'

Mallory nodded. 'You go first. I'm ready.'

'I can only imagine what she told you at the time. Throughout the years of our marriage I came to almost understand her devious mind. But this is the truth, Mallory. You *must* believe me.

'That time when I came home to Appleton a few days ahead of you, Suzannah phoned and asked me to meet her for dinner. She said she had something to tell me—about you. So I agreed. We met and had dinner. I could tell she was flirting with me—she always had but I'd never been interested in her. Never. It had been you who'd stolen my heart from the first time you'd looked at me with those incredible brown eyes of yours.

'Suzannah confessed that you were seeing another man in Brisbane and didn't know how to break it off with me. I told her that was hard to believe, considering we saw or spoke to each other nearly every day. She gave me his name, detailed times and dates of your alleged meetings.'

'Will Brannon,' Mallory whispered.

'Yes,' Nick agreed. 'I know it isn't true, Mallory, because when I returned to Brisbane, and you were refusing to see me, I cornered Will and asked him the truth. He denied it emphatically and provided evidence that he was, in fact, having an affair with one of his supervisors.'

'Yes. He was in a constant state of panic over it being discovered. They got married, you know, and have been together ever since.'

'Good for him,' Nick said without enthusiasm. 'As you'd probably related all of this to Suzannah, she'd managed to twist it around to make it look as though *you* were the one he was having the affair with. It made my blood boil when she told me and, after getting angry, I drank myself into a stupor. I know it was dumb but Suzannah kept supplying me with drink after drink, relating bits of gossip about your affair. Basically, she was getting me rip-roaring drunk and fuelling my anger.

'Finally, I told her that we should go. I was in no condition to drive and so she volunteered. After that, I can't remember anything. Believe me, I've tried, but the alcohol had done its job and completely numbed my brain cells. I woke up in my bed, stark naked, with a roaring hangover. There was black lingerie on the floor which Suzannah claimed was hers.'

Nick ran a hand through his hair. 'The evidence was against me. As far as I knew, I *had* betrayed you and slept with her. I didn't know what to do. Then I was told that Suzannah was pregnant and that the child was mine. You were refusing to even breathe the same air as me and abruptly moved to Sydney.'

Nick sat down and held her hand. 'Do you know, it was all a lie? She confessed, almost two years after we were married, when I found her in bed with my accountant and demanded a divorce. She said that I was out cold when we arrived back at my house. She undressed me, tangled the sheets, left the lingerie—everything. There was even lipstick on one of the champagne glasses I found beside the bed. We had never slept together. The pregnancy was a hoax and when the baby was due to begin showing she conveniently had a ''miscarriage''.'

They were both silent for a while before Mallory said, 'She was obsessed with you. When we first started dating—seriously dating—I asked Suzannah if it bothered her and she said no. She was happy for me. When we started talking *engagements*, I guess that's when she began to panic.' Mallory shook her head in stunned amazement. 'It all fits. All of the pieces. No wonder she protested about seeing my father for a pregnancy test. There was nothing to check. She supposedly bought the pregnancy test from an out-of-town chemist, performed the test herself and then called me with the result.'

'She wasn't pregnant,' Nick reiterated. 'When I found out I filed for a divorce immediately. I was surprised when she didn't contest my action but that was only because she had a plan of her own.'

'Rebekah?' Mallory guessed, and he nodded.

'This time Suzannah drugged my drink, ensuring that I wasn't too 'out of it' to get her pregnant. Again, I don't remember much about the night but the results were definitely conclusive this time around.'

'What about Rebekah? I mean…' Mallory hesitated. 'I don't want you to take this the wrong way or anything but…is…is she…?'

'Is Rebekah my daughter? You don't need to be shy in asking the question I asked the instant Suzannah told me she was pregnant. She'd had numerous affairs—too numerous to count. I requested DNA and blood tests to establish paternity when Rebekah was born. She's mine all right. Thank God for small miracles.' A smile broke through his pain.

'She's been everything to me, Mallory. I love her so intensely.' He squeezed her hand.

'It shows. You're a fantastic father, Nick.'

'I was ninety-nine per cent sure that she wasn't my baby, so when the test proved positive I felt as though I'd been given the most precious gift in the world. As I've told you before, I was caught up in the overseas professorship and basically had my hands tied. Arlene ensured that Suzannah made every single doctor's appointment and the obstetrician kept me well informed.

'Then, very soon after Rebekah was born, I had to go back and finish that tour. Leaving my beautiful baby girl was one of the hardest things I've ever had to do. The knowledge that Arlene was there to take care of her was my only consolation.'

'But what about Suzannah?' Mallory blurted out. 'I mean, didn't *she* care for Rebekah?'

Nick let go of her hand, his body tense. The last thing Mallory wanted to do was to cause him more pain, but it was necessary for both of them to get through this and then they could put it behind them—for ever.

'From the instant Rebekah was born, Suzannah declared she wanted nothing to do with her. She despised the fact that being pregnant almost ruined her figure and she flatly refused to breastfeed. So, from the moment she was born, Rebekah Mallory Sterling was handed over to Arlene. Yes.' He nodded. 'Suzannah insisted she be your namesake as a gentle reminder that you and I could never be together. She was wrong. Every time I looked at my daughter I saw hope of one day obtaining freedom. We both knew the only reason she'd decided to get pregnant was so I wouldn't divorce her. She was wrong. As soon as I returned from the travelling professorship I filed for divorce and custody of Rebekah.'

'And then Suzannah was killed.'

'Yes.' Nick sat down in a chair, his elbows resting on his knees. 'When I heard, all I felt was relief. The nightmare was over. She'd been out with her latest lover, drinking too much and driving too fast. Both of them were killed outright on impact.'

'It was a shock to me and I did grieve for the person I knew as my friend,' she told him softly. 'I was still so hurt and angry with you, Nick. I felt betrayed, and Suzannah had managed to keep that hurt and anger alive and festering within me. I knew if I went to her funeral that I'd give you a piece of my mind—and I didn't want to end up arguing over Suzannah's grave. It wouldn't have been right.

'She'd kept in close contact over the years, telling me that *you* were the one having affairs and not providing adequately for her. We spoke on the phone regularly and then there were her annual visits back—'

'Annual visits?' Nick interrupted her. 'Suzannah came back to Appleton? Regularly?'

Mallory frowned with surprise. 'Yes. Once a year she'd come and spend about a week with me. The only year she didn't come was when she was pregnant with Rebekah. She said she didn't feel up to travelling as she suffered from motion sickness, but the year after that certainly made up for it as she brought Rebekah with her.'

'She did *what*?' Nick stood up, his hands clenched by his sides. 'How old was Rebekah?'

'Two months. They only stayed for three nights instead of a week that time as Rebekah was unsettled. Now that you've told me that Arlene cared for the baby since her birth, it's no wonder Suzannah seemed unable to tend the poor darling. She refused point blank to let me help and

ended up calling me all sorts of names.' Mallory shrugged.
'At the time I put it down to postnatal depression.'

'I can well believe the name-calling. She had quite a
repertoire. Once a year she would tell Arlene she was visiting her parents and did indeed, take Rebekah with her,
telling Arlene that a nanny would be employed to care for
the baby. Instead, she returned here and stayed with you.'
He nodded, as though that explained everything.

'Yes. I thought you knew. You were usually overseas at
a conference.' Mallory could tell Nick's mind was working
in overdrive.

'She'd come back here, sprouting her lies about how
wonderful our marriage was, wouldn't she?'

'Well, yes, generally.' Mallory looked down at her
hands.

'It all makes perfect sense now.'

'What does?' She eyed him warily.

'The fact that you'd never once tried to contact me. I
knew in the beginning that you were mad with me and I
didn't blame you. The odds were definitely stacked against
me but I thought after a year or so that you'd contact me,
give me a chance to explain. Instead, the only news I heard
about you was from contact with your brother, Jeff.'

'Jeff? He never said anything about you.'

'Tactful man, your brother. I never directly asked about
you but Jeff knew the score. He'd volunteer any information on what you were currently up to and it gave me great
pleasure to hear about your thriving and successful practice
here in Appleton.

'I knew you didn't hold grudges for long and therefore
was quite surprised when you didn't contact me. I started
to grow quite bitter towards you and even thought I'd misjudged your character. The bitterness continued to grow so
that after the first year of marriage to Suzannah, when she'd

emotionally recovered from her ''miscarriage'', the thought of filing for a divorce seemed, well, not that necessary.

'Suzannah and I lived our separate lives at separate ends of the house. Although it was difficult to come to terms with, I began to believe that you hadn't really loved me. You appeared to have forgotten me altogether and it didn't do much for my ego. But when Suzannah confessed to everything I knew I needed a divorce—for my *own* sanity. Now I discover that you did love me but all the time had Suzannah manipulating you with her lies, telling you that she and I were happy.'

'Well, mostly. She told me that you'd had affairs but that she forgave you because she loved you so much. I guess it was her way of making sure I stayed loyal to her and wouldn't contact you. The fact that you'd supposedly betrayed *me* with *her* only added weight to her story of your affairs.'

Nick was speechless. He gathered Mallory closer to him and held her very tightly, as though he would never let her go—ever again. Suzannah had done an excellent job of ruining both their lives.

'We have each other now, Mallory,' Nick finally spoke. 'We've found each other once again—at last. The past two years have been good for me. I've managed to put my life back into perspective, and when I saw you at the retrieval team competition I knew the time was right to come home.'

'And now here we are.' Mallory looked at him and smiled. She was exhausted, relieved and happy. 'I feel that Suzannah has gone, Nick. She's messed up too many years of our lives—let's let her go, once and for all.'

Nick turned to face her. 'Once and for all,' he repeated, and lowered his lips to hers.

The kiss was one of relief. Finally, they could allow their true feelings to flow freely, to be honest with each other and to allow their love the freedom to grow.

'Mallory, I do love you.' Nick pulled away and looked at her, his eyes alight with desire and promise. He kissed her briefly once more. 'We're going to have such a wonderful life together. You, me, Rebekah and all the other children we'll have. We'll fill that big house with such sunshine and radiance and...' He trailed off when Mallory shook her head and stood up.

'There's more, Nick.' Her voice was a choked whisper, all happiness wiped from her face.

'Mallory?'

She turned away from the worry in his tone, trying to control the tears threatening behind her eyes. She heard him stand and felt his warm hands on her shoulders as he turned her around.

'What is it?' he asked gently. 'If we can survive everything Suzannah has done to us, we can survive *anything*.'

'Oh, Nick, I hope so.' Mallory swallowed a sob, trying to summon the courage to confess the truth.

He went to envelop her in his arms but she held up a hand to stop him.

'No.' She needed to see his face when she told him the terrible news, to try and read his initial reaction. 'Nick, I can't have children.' There, she'd told him. The millisecond of relief she felt was squashed by the immediate devastation that crossed his face.

'What? How?' he questioned. 'But I know you *want* children, Mal.'

'I do, Nick.' She clasped her hands to her chest, covering her heart. 'More than anything in the world, I would love to have a child to grow within me, but it's medically impossible.'

'The accident,' he whispered, and she nodded.

'My pelvis was so drastically crushed that my reproductive organs don't function as they should.'

He was silent for quite a while and Mallory willed him

to speak—to say anything. Was he angry? Upset? Finally, he cleared his throat.

'That evening a few weeks ago when we went for the picnic—it was this that made you so upset, wasn't it?'

She nodded. 'I...I didn't know how to tell you. I know how desperately you want more children, Nick, but I...I...can't.' Mallory's voice choked on a sob.

Nick held her securely in his arms. 'I'll be honest with you, Mallory. I'm stunned.' He pulled back a little and looked down at her. 'When I think of what you've been through with that terrible accident and it's hurting you once again.' He kissed her lips and then released her. 'I need to...go.'

Mallory wrapped her arms around herself, feeling bereft.

'I still love you and we will still be together, but at the moment I just need time to...come to terms with this information. The walk home will do me good,' he added, as though remembering they'd arrived in her car and his was still at the clinic.

Mallory could only nod at his words. Nick must have read the pain and mortification on her face because he came and placed a quick kiss on her lips, before turning and walking out of the door.

Mallory stayed where she was. Unable to move. Feeling dead inside.

She must have stood there for at least ten long minutes, replaying the conversation in her head. Wondering whether there had been a better way to tell him.

For a man who so dearly loved his daughter and so desperately wanted to have more children to bring him equally as much joy, Mallory knew her declaration had devastated him. He'd said they'd still be together, but right at this moment Mallory had doubts that he'd be able to come to terms with it.

Her knees gave way, tired of holding her up, and she

slumped to the floor. The old feelings of helplessness returned and Mallory began to weep. She had always yearned to be a mother. The maternal feelings were so much a part of her. Rebekah filled her heart with love and happiness and Mallory didn't know how she would cope if that one thread of life was ripped from her grasp.

As she sat there she prayed that somehow, by some miracle, things would turn out right. They just had to.

The ringing of the phone pulled her from the deep sleep she was in and for a moment Mallory had no idea where she was. The only thing she knew for sure was that she was very uncomfortable.

Opening her eyes, she tried to stand, but found that her legs were curled beneath her on the floor. Using her arms, Mallory hoisted her body up and managed to quickly make it across the room to the phone, which was on the table beside her favourite chair, before her legs gave way again.

'Hello,' she mumbled, her throat dry and scratchy. 'Dr Newman.'

'Mallory.' Nick's deep voice rumbled down the line and Mallory almost dropped the receiver.

'Nick,' she whispered. All coherent thought left her as their discussion the previous evening came flooding back.

'Mallory, we need to talk.' He was direct and to the point. 'Can you come over? Rebekah would love to see you,' he added as an incentive.

Anger burst forth inside her as she gripped the receiver more tightly. 'Stop using Rebekah as a weapon, Nick. You've done it from the very beginning. Well, it won't work this time. I think it's best for Rebekah if I don't see her again.'

'I can understand your anger—' Nick ventured but, Mallory interrupted.

'Oh, you can, can you? I don't think so, Nick. Do you

have any idea how hard it was for me to confess that to you last night? How I depended upon your strength in my time of need? If this is how you react to emotional situations then I think it better for both of us that we *don't* marry. It will save us a lot of heartache.'

'You're overreacting. We need to talk,' he said again.

'I have nothing more to say to you, Nick.'

'Then just listen. I love you, Mallory. *Please*,' he implored. 'Come over. Arlene's gone down to Brisbane for the weekend to visit a friend so it will be just the three of us.'

Mallory was silent. She'd never heard Nick so worried, or so desperate.

'Please? Don't deny me the chance to explain—*again*.'

She looked at the clock on the wall. Almost seven a.m. She couldn't believe she'd slept in a crumpled heap on the floor, but her clothing attested to it as she was still wearing what she'd put on yesterday morning.

Finally she spoke. 'I'll be there for lunch.' Although every fibre in her being begged to go to him immediately, Mallory wanted him to wait. Suffer a little as he'd made her suffer last night.

'But—'

'I have house calls to make. I'll be there for lunch.'

'Sounds great.' The pleasant tone in his voice was forced. 'I'll have lunch ready and waiting.'

'Good.' And with that she put the phone down. Her hand was shaking. What had she done? Was her stubborn pride going to ruin everything? Why didn't she just go to him?

No. Mallory took a deep breath and stood, commanding her legs to hold her weight. Nick had called the shots since his arrival only a few short weeks ago. Not this time.

Mallory showered and dressed, before ensuring she had everything she needed in her medical bag. As she visited little Nathan Hone, whose ear infection was clearing up nicely, she found herself constantly looking at her watch.

'Is anything wrong?' Chloe asked.

'No.' Mallory forced a smile. 'Just a lot to get through today. I'll call in and see him next week. You've got your six-week postnatal check soon and appear to be coping brilliantly so you're in the clear.'

'Great,' Chloe replied as Mallory waved goodbye.

Next was Rose whose recovery had been unremarkable, a good sign. Mallory knew that Nick had seen Rose in his clinic earlier the previous week, and although she'd received a written report, stating that Rose was doing exceptionally well, it was good to see it for herself.

'Every day I feel stronger and can do more. Soon I'll be back in Arthur's way, complaining and nagging at him again.'

'And I look forward to it, dear,' Arthur replied, and bent to kiss his wife who was sitting in a comfortable chair in the lounge room.

Again Mallory found herself clock-watching, her internal nervousness growing with every passing minute. Soon she would see Nick and her heartbeat was all a-flutter. She knew they'd patch things up but making him wait was important to her.

When she pulled her car into Jessie McFarland's driveway she could see the old woman walking towards her.

'What do you think you're doing here?' she spluttered as Mallory climbed out of her car.

'I've come to give you your check-up. Just like I always do.'

'Get back in that car of yours and get off to Nicholas Sterling's house.'

'But…' Mallory stopped, unsure what Jessie meant.

'I've just had him on the phone in a complete tither. I've never heard a man so agitated.'

'Wh-what did he say?'

'He wanted to know whether you were here and how much longer you'd be. When I asked him why, he told me he's about to propose to you and that you're purposely making him wait.'

Mallory lifted her chin defiantly. 'So?'

'I'd swear...' Jessie shook her head in bemusement '...that you're from my own blood, you're so pertinacious at times. Go to the man,' she ordered, waving her walking stick in the air. 'He's waited over five years for you and you for him. Stop being so stubborn and let the poor man propose.'

Mallory looked at Jessie and shook her head. 'I'm scared,' she confessed.

'And so you should be.' Jessie's tone was gentler. 'You're in love. You're wondering whether you have the guts to take on this lifelong commitment and make it work. You're wondering whether he'll react to everything the way he's done now you've told him you can't have kiddies.'

'How? Did he...?'

'No, he didn't tell me. It was obvious when he called that things had been straightened out between the two of you. I guessed. Just let me give you some advice.' Jessie came to stand beside Mallory and put her hand on her shoulder.

'You'll work it out, ''work'' being the operative word. You'll get to know each other better and will be able to improve the good qualities and strengthen the weaknesses. You've worked out so much to get to this point, there's no stopping either of you now.

'Besides, that little girl needs you.'

'I need her,' Mallory acknowledged. 'But I need her father, too.'

'Then what in the world are you doing here? Go, child. I understand you wanting to make the man wait, but enough's enough. Go—with my blessing—and start a new life with the man of your dreams.'

Mallory gave Jessie a quick hug. 'Thanks. I think I might just do that.'


'How much longer, Becka?' Nick asked the little girl as they sat playing on the floor with some blocks. 'How much longer?'

Mallory had quietly let herself into the house and gone in search of them. Nick had his back to her, playing intently with his daughter, mindful of the plaster cast on her leg.

Mallory's heart swelled with love for him at the caring and patient attitude he displayed with Rebekah. He loved that little girl so much that she should have known the shock that she couldn't give him any more children would have taken a little time to adjust to.

He built up a tower and Rebekah knocked it down with her hand. Her little blue eyes spied Mallory in the doorway and her face radiated happiness.

'Malwee,' she squealed.

Mallory crossed to her side and bent to hug her. 'Hello, sweetie,' she crooned, and gave Rebekah a kiss. 'I can see you're doing very well. You look so much better.'

'You're here.' Nick put out a hand to touch her hair. 'I'm not imagining it?'

'I'm really here, Nick.' Mallory's gaze met his.

Rebekah clutched at Mallory's hand. 'Play with Becka. Daddy, Malwee's come to play.'

'Yes, she has.' Nick's smile was enormous and it filled Mallory with happiness. Everything would be all right. She'd known it before she'd arrived but now she *felt* it.

'Play with blocks,' Rebekah ordered, and Mallory sat down on the floor beside the blocks.

'That's an A,' Rebekah announced, holding up the appropriate block. 'That's a G,' she told them earnestly.

'Can you build a tower?' Nick asked. 'Get Mallory to help you,' he decided. 'I bet she loves building towers.'

'I do,' Mallory declared, and together she and Rebekah built a big tower before it fell to the ground. Blocks went everywhere and Mallory started to gather them up again, delighting in the child's giggles. That was when she realised exactly what Nick was doing.

He'd arranged some blocks to spell out a message. Mallory was immediately thankful that she was already sitting down.

There, in multicoloured plastic, he'd put the letters together to spell out, WILL YOU MARRY ME.

Mallory could only stare at the letters, her eyes beginning to blur with tears. She looked at him and then at Rebekah, who seemed oblivious to the adults around her, then back to Nick again.

'I'm sorry, Mallory,' he whispered, and took her hand in his. 'It came as a shock and I didn't handle it well. If we can't have any children, that's fine. We have Rebekah but, more important, we have each other. We can try GIFT, IVF, adoption,' he continued earnestly. 'As long as we're *together*, that's all that matters. Please, Mallory—marry me. Become my wife. Become Rebekah's mother.'

Nick tenderly wiped the tears from her eyes, a look of hope on his face. Mallory looked at the blocks, unable to believe that this moment was finally here. He was waiting. Waiting for her answer.

Reaching out her free hand, she gathered three blocks together and arranged them. Y… E… S… was what they spelt.

A slow smile spread across Nick's face, his eyes alight with love as he came closer to claim her lips in a kiss.

'Kiss Becka, too, Daddy,' the little girl interrupted, and Nick laughed.

Mallory also laughed as he complied with the wish of

the other female in his life. Mallory felt incredible—on top of the world—and it was all because of the two people in front of her.

'Mallory is going to come and live with us,' Nick told Rebekah.

'Yippee,' Rebekah said loudly.

'My sentiments exactly.' Nick nodded.

# EPILOGUE

'REBEKAH MALLORY STERLING,' Mallory warned in a voice her daughter had come to learn and respect over the past three years.

'Yes, Mummy?' the five-and-a-half-year-old asked innocently.

'You've been told countless times before not to climb up on your bookshelves. Thank goodness your father bolted them to the wall after your previous fall or there would have been another.'

'Sorry, Mummy.'

'All right. Go and wash your hands, please. It's time for dinner and Arlene is waiting.'

'Yes, Mummy,' Rebekah replied with resignation, but before she'd taken more than a step towards the bathroom a baby's cry echoed throughout the house. 'He's awake, Mummy. Edward's awake.'

Rebekah bounded out of her room, Mallory hard on her heels. 'Quietly, Becka,' she suggested, but knew it was no use. Four-month-old Edward Fitzwilliam Sterling was the apple of his big sister's eye.

Mallory entered the bedroom she shared with her husband and crossed to Edward's cot. She still preferred to have him close during the evenings, making it much easier for feeding.

'You can't be hungry *again*,' she said to her son, but his cries continued.

'Can I hold him, please, Mummy? He always stops crying when *I* hold him.'

It was true. Edward clearly adored his big sister, and although he wasn't a troublesome baby his cries were very loud.

'All right. Sit down on the bed and get comfortable.'

Rebekah did as she was told, making sure she had a pillow to support Edward's weight.

'There you are.' Mallory kissed her son's forehead, before placing him in his sister's waiting arms. Within seconds his cries abated and he opened his eyes to gaze at Rebekah.

Mallory perched herself beside them, putting her arm around Rebekah's shoulders.

'You're such a wonderful sister, Rebekah, and a very big help to me. Thank you, darling.' She kissed her daughter's head.

'My family,' a deep male voice said from the doorway.

'You're home early,' Mallory said, her face lighting up with delight at seeing her husband. Nick crossed to her side and kissed her, then Rebekah and his son.

'Thankfully,' he groaned. 'I didn't think surgery would ever finish. It was one complication after another today, but finally we managed to wade through them. How was your clinic this morning?'

'Busy, but I managed to get home before Rebekah finished school. I must confess to enjoying my two mornings per week, consulting, although most of the time it stretches well into the afternoon.'

'Dr Jayton is an excellent general practitioner, Mal.'

'I know and I'm glad I can trust her with my practice. Perhaps once Edward is at school I'll go back to working longer hours, but until then…' She let her sentence trail off as both of them knew what she was getting at. Family came first. Especially after everything they'd endured to have one.

Becoming pregnant with Edward hadn't been easy. After

almost two years of IVF the test had finally come back positive but her obstetrician had prescribed complete bed-rest for the duration of her pregnancy. It had nearly driven Mallory around the twist but every time she looked at her baby boy she knew it had been worth it.

Her obstetrician had also warned against any further pregnancies, due to the strain the baby had put on her pelvis. For that reason Edward had been delivered by a pre-arranged Caesarean section.

Having more children wasn't an option—the risk was too great to Mallory's health. They had one of each—and that was more than Mallory had thought she'd ever have.

'So, now, Mrs Sterling,' Nick said as he pulled her to her feet, 'are you ready to go on holidays?'

Mallory wrapped her arms around his waist and snuggled against him. She loved him so completely. Her one true love—and she had the rest of her life to spend with him and their children.

'I'm more than ready to go on holidays, but I have a suggestion for you.'

'Hmm?' he queried as he watched his daughter, kissing her little brother. 'What might that be?'

'That we fly off into the sunset—and leave the mobile phones at home.'

'Brilliant, Mrs Sterling. Absolutely brilliant!'

# MILLS & BOON®

*Makes any time special*™

**Mills & Boon publish 29 new titles every month. Select from...**

Modern Romance™          Tender Romance™

Sensual Romance™

Medical Romance™   Historical Romance™

MAT2

# 4 FREE
### books and a surprise gift!

We would like to take this opportunity to thank you for reading this Mills & Boon® book by offering you the chance to take FOUR more specially selected titles from the Medical Romance™ series absolutely FREE! We're also making this offer to introduce you to the benefits of the Reader Service™—

- ★ FREE home delivery
- ★ FREE gifts and competitions
- ★ FREE monthly Newsletter
- ★ Exclusive Reader Service discounts
- ★ Books available before they're in the shops

Accepting these FREE books and gift places you under no obligation to buy, you may cancel at any time, even after receiving your free shipment. Simply complete your details below and return the entire page to the address below. *You don't even need a stamp!*

**YES!** Please send me 4 free Medical Romance books and a surprise gift. I understand that unless you hear from me, I will receive 6 superb new titles every month for just £2.40 each, postage and packing free. I am under no obligation to purchase any books and may cancel my subscription at any time. The free books and gift will be mine to keep in any case.

M0ZEA

Ms/Mrs/Miss/Mr ...............................Initials...........................................
BLOCK CAPITALS PLEASE

Surname ........................................................................................................

Address ........................................................................................................

............................................................................................................................

.......................................................Postcode..................................

**Send this whole page to:**
**UK: FREEPOST CN81, Croydon, CR9 3WZ**
**EIRE: PO Box 4546, Kilcock, County Kildare (stamp required)**

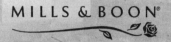